# Don't Dig Me Any Deeper

# By lopez sands

Published by LopezHook productions
www.lopezhook.webs.com
© 2013



9 781257 902712
ISBN 978-1-257-90271-2
90000

**Introduction:**

On my drive back into the city U-Haul attached, boxes packed, it just seemed all this had to be unreal, coming home again. Coming back to Chicago, in March, one of the coldest months of March I could remember.  The city seemed to be stuck under a thousand blankets of unwanted cold and snow.  The people I passed, emerging from some awkward form of hibernation.  I never thought I would be doing this, moving back to the city which had taken so much from me. Chicago at one time was a like a torturous dream that seemed to never end, the failures with my parents, the failures with love.  If I had not moved away, the downward spiral I was on would have sent me six feet under. Moving to Baltimore wasn't my brightest idea but it had worked out well.  I had been doing exactly what I wanted, writing and learning so much about myself putting behind the misery of no acceptance and leaning to love myself, something few people accomplish in a life time.  Now all I could feel was a sense of lost, betrayal and anger.

I begin working freelance for various papers when I arrived in Atlanta over ten years ago.  After working my ass off around town the Atlanta Journal finally gave me a break, eventually inviting me to be part of their team.  Now here I was returning to the windy city to try to rebuild my life.  I actually believe this was a process I would never have to do again.  Sure I had my ups and downs but I was happy.  Aries made me happy.  I didn't set my happiness up on his back but he was an essential part of my life.  A great part of my life was taken away with a whisper, a sound and the red.  Maybe I came back because I had to run. Maybe I wanted to put the rest of the ghosts of my past, so that I could live with my present pain.  Or, just maybe I was running away from the memories of the south into someplace that was familiar. Who knows, I surely didn't, all I know is that things were just working out this way.

I had met my heart in Atlanta.  That's what I would remember most about that city, along with the high murder rate and the beautiful black men you see, even f the were as lost as any other black man in this country. I remember the day I met Aries Kelly, it is still so clear.  At this moment everyday felt like yesterday, every memory as if it had just happened.  My mind was on a constant replay.  The first day we met, I was working on a story about what police was calling a serial killer that was working the Atlanta.  The national press was ignoring it but since it was being downplayed by the police commissioner and the mayor it wasn't much of a surprise.  They would not even admit to a connection among the murders until someone started an internet site.  I approached my boss and told him it was time we printed something on the story because so many young black men were being murdered

"Young black men die everyday in this city, what's your point", Bill asked.  He was right of course but I pushed the issue and told him random violence is not something we could control or inform the citizens on but someone who is targeting specific people, we can at least warn people.

If they were white, would we would even be having this conversation, I asked.  The first story was published a week later.  Part of the story was talking to community leaders, so I called one of the service centers and arranged to do an interview with Aries; he worked as director of UNITY, which was in the heart of the city.  When I saw him I knew that I was in trouble. He wasn't the ebony poster child but his smile did something inside me.  It stole my breath from me.  He was the most beautiful man I had ever laid eyes on.  He was just so, soon. Words can hardly describe him but I guess they'll have to do. Tall, looking up at him from my five ten frame, I almost forgot why I was there.  Slender, not skinny but toned with a bald head and all.  The graze of facial hair on his face was placed every so nicely, chiseled jaw, perfectly intertwined in with his full lips.  He had on shades when I walked in his office for the first time, I remember wondering what his eyes looked like and why inside. When he removed his glasses and stood to shake my hand, he smiled and his eyes widen in response, my heart stopped at that moment.  A light shade of brown that me know I was a goner from that very moment.  It was a face that you might see several times and each time you find something new, something fascinating, something memorable each time you looked at him. "You there", he asked, as he laughed slightly that echoed around the room but to the depths of my soul.

After we finished our interview I thought that would be last time I saw him but a few days later, after the first article came out, he called me at the office and asked if he could take me to dinner to thank me for covering the story.  I tried to get out of going, even though I wanted to have dinner with him.  He frightened me.  Somewhere inside my soul, I knew that the person God had planned for me rested in his body and when that idea came into my head my only response was to run.  I had long ago given up on the idea of love.  He didn't take no for an answer, but then again I ever quite said no, I don't think I could.  He made me laugh and I hadn't done that a very long time.  I was always so damn serious.  All I had done sense I arrived in Atlanta was throw myself into work, trying to prove to myself and prove my father wrong, he had said my life would amount to nothing, that I was a forsaken soul.  I had been ATL for a year with a VCR and an IPOD as my only friends.  With friends like Lena, Billie and Mary J you hardly noticed that spending cold days at work and even colder nights alone in bed.  My fridge was filled with carrots, crackers, bottle of white wine, bottles of water, pancake mix, syrup and three week outdated milk and my life had been filled with even less. I had taken my work to bed every night in that year, but it hardly keeps me warm.  In college I tried so many warm bodies to keep me warm that I had decided to find out who I was and until I knew that I knew I was never going to be good for anyone else.

At dinner we talked and Aries told me about growing upon Atlanta and I told him about Chicago.  Our lives hadn't been that different at least in the early years, raised by religious parents, finding out that our attraction was for men but at some point, his parents accepted him and I keep my secret.  Aries grew up never looking for love and I grew up thinking love was some manufactured idea for people to make money from. When I look back that was the first brick around my heart, because I didn't believe someone could love me or that maybe I was being punished for who I loved, especially when it cost me the relationship with my parents. I had learned that your heart could be fragile and the only way to save it was to brick it up but maybe I had caused it to lose oxygen and die.  Aries on the other hand loved the search because "it's the journey", he'd say, "that made love worth keeping."  I still didn't buy his little speech that night and the more he tugged at my heart, the more I pulled away.  Then he looked me in the eyes and said,

"What good is a heart if it isn't allowed to beat"?  I was hooked and for the next ten years, we were inseparable.  He's gone now and now I needed to get away.  I needed a change. My heart had been smashed into a million little pieces and each piece reminded me of the good times.  I was coming home again.  When people say you can never go home again, it's not the place, it's the feelings.

As I drove up to my apartment, my brother Michael sat on the porch.  He looked up when he saw the car tires stop in front of house.  He smiled, still the egghead he had always been.  He was always supportive of me.  The look in his eyes mad this a lot easier.  They still carried those pouches underneath them and the smile he had that brought the wrinkles right above his nose and around his mouth.  His chin jostled out which such force, highlighting his strength. I was happy to see him.  He had never disappointed me, he was always my protector.  He still stood taller than the heavens to me.  He has never been too hung up on his body, probably because no matter what he ate, it never made him less attractive.  I, on the other hand, had to use the gym on regular bases.  Michael was never a small boy, he just happens to part of the lucky selection of people who managed a gym body without a gym anywhere nearby. He had no stomach but lost of time, his head was larger than anyone in our family, and he looked more like our father than I did from the oversized nose to the large forehead.

Michael walks up to me and I could see his breath as he made his way closer.  His oversized parker wrapping his shivering body,

"Well it's about damn time you showed up, I though you got lost," he said.

Michael it's good to see you too.  There was a brief silence that lasted longer in my head than in real time. Then Michael wrapped me in his arms.

"I'm sorry I didn't make it to Aries funeral, I…"

… Enough said. I know you would if you could.

"Thanks, listen Kim and I fixed up the place with the things you shipped."

How is that beautiful wife of yours?

"Just fine, she's just fine."
Michael had married a fine lady and his wedding was the first time I had seen my parents. I wanted to ask how mom and dad were but that damn pride had swelled up to quickly to allow even that question; I guess I did inherit something from my father.

Michael and I entered the townhouse, I looked around at the wonderful job, I'm sure Kim did alone. It felt good to be at home, or at least in place that was familiar. I walked around, looking at the place, the painting over the fireplace of two African soldiers holding each other in battle. Aries had brought it for me on our first anniversary.

> *"I am your friend, your boy, your nigga, your lover but most of all I am your soldier. I will be there for every battle and by your side for ever war. I will fight for you, for us and for our love until the day that I die",*

That is what the card read. Tears begin to drip slowly from my eyes, before I could wipe them away, Michael saw them and didn't say a word, and he just reached his arm around me and pulled me close. This was the first time I had felt safe and I broke down for the first time since Aries death and I wept.

When I woke up it was eleven at night and I checked to make sure all the doors were locked and then I begin to unpack and put away a few things and move some things around. I put on some Nina Simone and poured myself a glass of red wine and walked around the house. I pulled out the photo album of what seemed to be someone else life. It was hard to imagine living my life without Aries. It had been one year, three months and four days since his death but time hadn't been my friend; it had kept me in a vacuum of sadness. The house was silent and even Nina couldn't change that. You can never understand emptiness until your life is filled with hopes, dreams and love and then it is taken away from you. I came across one of the first letters Aries ever wrote me, he use to love to write to me.

> *"To my friend, my boy, my baby,*
> *The time is now that I take time to let you know what is good with me. Boss, my spirit speaks to all the order of divinity, be it whatever, man, my soul rejoices in the*

The emptiness feels so heavy that all the strength you had can never ever lift the loneliness off your chest.  No one can understand that.  I once heard someone say that it's harder to see a person you love and know you can never be with him or her, and then it is to know you can never see him or her because at least you realize it wasn't their choice.  No, it definitely harder to know that you can never hear their voice, you can never feel their touch or feel their heart beat or come alive when they smile at you.  To realize that love will never be waiting for you at home, after the world had beaten you, no it is the worst sadness of all because, it's the one, even in sleep, you can never change that emptiness.

Kim and Michael stopped by the next morning waking me from my deep sleep.  There I was on the couch holding the picture of Aries and his letter when Kim shook me and told me to get my ass up and give her some love.  She was so sweet.  My brother had kissed a lit of women to find the jewel she was. He always said he would know when he had found the one and I guess Kim was the one.  She stood there smiling at me from her five foot five frame, dressed in her plain white dress that buttoned down the front.  She had the knack for making the simplest outfit look as it was made by the hottest designer. Her bug eyes lit with love, her nose and mouth added to her beauty.  She wasn't the typical Hollywood beauty that often is the magazine favorite; she was actually more beautiful in her uniqueness of facial features. Her hair dreaded back in a ponytail and her black strapped sandals attached made her legs seem longer than they actually were. Even the slight dark patched that covered her knees seems to blend in to this exquisite beauty. When I first met Kim her hands caught my attention, they were so neat, long fingers and nails just an inch longer from her fingertips. Kim was pure lady. Here I stood now, not really knowing her like I should have but somehow the connection was still there. We use to talk on the phone for hours because I avoided coming back to Chicago unless it was absolutely necessary. Our relationship was mostly built on phone calls, Christmas and birthday cards and pictures.

She and Michael made a few trips to Atlanta where they met Aries. Michael had his doubts about Aries but Kim was our biggest supporter. Michael believed Aries was too profile in the community and even knowing that I was not about to hide who I was at this point in my life it still bothered him that Aries was well, so out. Kim knew we worked. She saw the love. Michael eventually came around, to this day I still have no idea what changed, but on one of their visits him and Aries made a trip to the store insisting that Kim and I stay behind. For close to two hours, no word from them. We just knew Michael had said something offensive and Aries manhood was challenge and we would get a call to bail them out of jail. As I look back, I understand that what drew me to Aries was that he and Michael were alike in many ways, strong willed, stubborn, kind hearted to a fault and they both made me fill safe. When they finally returned they were all smiles, laughing like old friends. All Michael said was he thought Aries was a great guy and I was lucky to have him in my life.

Here I am staring at my sister in law; they were here to take me to breakfast so I went. I really had no other choice. We went to the Pancake House in Hyde Park. She was telling me all about her new job; she was appointed coordinator of the education taskforce for the mayor. She was so proud. She and Michael were thinking of having their first child. I mentioned that I thought she might be pregnant; she had a glow about her. She laughed and was assured me she wasn't.

"I told mom and dad that you were moving back," Michael said.  This kind of killed the good vibration.

Why did you do a thing like that?  He was speechless.

What did they say?  He sat silently, this said enough to me.  It didn't matter it's not like I expected them to accept me with open arms.  No they would continue to act as if I didn't exist the way they have for so many years.

"Well on to brighter things," Kim changes the subject, "We invited a few people over tonight to sort of welcome you home."

I'm really not in the mood…

"…Nothing major, just a few friends," she says.  We sat at the table eating our pancakes, laughing occasionally and catching up on things in our life.  Aries name came up a few times and the silence brought me back to my existence. It was hard, I wanted to remember Aries, the love we shared, the family we had built together but it was hard. He was a part of my soul and that would never change.  Somewhere inside me I knew it was time to let him go, he would want that.  I told myself moving on did not mean forgetting him because as long as I lived, he lived. If I stopped living now, then his memories would die with me.  If I gave up on life, the bastard who took him away would be triumphant.  He had took away Aries physically but he could never take what we shared, the good the bad, he could never take away my heart.

After I showered, I turned on the radio and begin to listen as GCI played the same old bland top forty music.  I didn't mind that this generation idea of good music was derivative Chris Brown or new ways to describe how you get head but come on.  The sad thing was that was about the best in radio stations that this town had to offer. I turned on my CD player and listened to Maxwell's latest CD, the last time I danced with Aries, Maxwell serenaded us.  I was in his arms as the words carried us both. *If it's cool, we could do a little something, something*, Maxwell sand as I looked up into his eyes and he leant down and kissed me.  My heart still beat even after ten years in anticipation of making love to him, our lips connected and lit up our souls like two thousand pounds of dynamite, exploding with every flicker of our tongues.

"Gabriel", he whispered, "I love you".  Everything inside me ached.  Every ounce of my flesh came alive as his hands touched parts of my body. With every glide of his hand I became more aware of myself. I don't think I had ever been that aware of anything until that moment. I looked up into his eyes and saw what lit my universe; I kissed him, our lip not parting seeming to be stuck together. The music, the smell calling me into him and I could not refuse the request which was made clear with the thrust of his tongue, it was an enchanting moment.

I finished dressing and went downstairs to wait for Michael to pick me up.  I had told him I would drive but he insisted that I let him pick me up; his excuse was he wanted to me to have a good time and not drink and drive. When my doorbell finally rang I had been sitting waiting for thirty minutes, Michael knew how I felt about being on time.

You're late, I said as I swung open the door.

"Sorry", said a voice with a smile on his face, "but better late than never. What you don't remember me?"

Of course I do. Simon, how are you?  Here I was looking at my first love, Simon Bennett and he still took my breath away even more than fifteen years later.

"The question is how you are?"

I'm good. We hug, then I stand back to look at him.  The first time I saw him, he made me feel the beat of my heart the first time and maturity had done him well.  He still had those glistening hazel eyes; I use to write poetry about him when I was fourteen.  When I was twelve my brother brought home this freshman not knowing how he would complicate my life.

"I missed you", he says as he reaches out and touches my face.

Really, there is this invention called the telephone, you heard of it right.

"Still the same smart ass, I see."

Why change a good thing.
My first love, my first piece of ass, this smooth yellow angel had been my first everything. We held a lot of secrets together; he preferred it that way, convincing me that it had to stay like that. I was his guilty pleasure as he paraded around with various females, but I was young and with youth comes stupidity.

"You ready to go?'

Sure, let me grab my keys.  A smile crept across my face as I turned around t grab my keys from the table.

On the drive we talked about nothing really.  We both were avoiding the real subject.  We mostly talked about Atlanta, the city, how Chicago had changed and joked about some funny childhood memories.  When he did bring up Aries, I noticed his face turned more intense, so I told him.  When he looked over at me his eyes still had the same glimmer that would make me melt, his hair was a lot shorter, probably trying to hide that receding hair line.  When he smiled at me or laughed I felt alive again, his voice was deep and just sort of rolled into me smoothly as thunder does on a stormy nights still managing to soothe you all at once. I felt a slight rumble inside.  From day one I was his captive audience.  He still bites his lower lip when he is in the midst of a conversation when he was censoring his self.

What's on your mind?
"You think you know me so well."
You're biting your lip.
"Michael knows everything about us."
You told him.
"About six years ago, I was drinking, actually I was pretty fucked up, separating from my wife, bad time and just came pouring out."
What hey, when we were teenagers, I was fucking your little brother.
"Something like that."
Sorry.
"No, I was an ass to you, I did feel guilty about the way it ended but it ended because I felt guilty."
I wasn't a child.
"Yes, you were. You were fourteen, I was eighteen."
What did he say?
"Pretty cool about it, not as shocked as I thought he would be.  Just so you can know, you're the one person I never regretted being with."
Thanks, We're here. I didn't want to relive that time in my life. I had made peace with it and going back to drudge up all the pain anger and even the joys would only disturb it.

As we entered the house with so many unfamiliar faces, I felt myself wanting to grab a hold of Simon and let me guide me through the maze of bodies and smiles but I kept thinking to myself which one is his wife. Michael called me not long after I moved to Atlanta to tell me that he was marrying some girl from the neighborhood.  I couldn't recall her and frankly I didn't give a damn.  I walked in front of Simon, every now and again looking back to make sure he was still behind me, he was. I walked and people spoke but I couldn't place many faces.  Was I totally blocking out my past.  No I couldn't be it still haunted my soul.  It was just another lifetime and I had tried so hard to think about the life I had been forced to abandon. I felt like an alien trying to blend into another species and no matter how they recognized me as one of their own, it could not hide how uncomfortable I felt. I spot Kim over by table still putting the food together or was she just adding more.  It didn't matter, the quicker she put it out the faster it seemed to disappear.   She sees me and stretches out her hands, we embrace.  She is dressed in a long black dress the clings to her delicate body, her hair dangling behind her the elegant hostess.

The rest of the night I walk through the crowd talking and reintroducing myself into this life.  I avoid Simon as much as I can, he stops occasionally to gage my mood but I would simply answer fine and trot off.  The music plays from the stereo in full force.  Oldies mixed with a few modern beats fill the air and the crowd seems to be guided by the intensity of the air. There is so much nonverbal language in the room; you can see it in their eyes and bodies.   The slight touches on elbows, or arms, the leans toward or away from those they speak to. Soon the rooms begin to empty and only a few brave more relaxed souls occupy the space. I see Simon as he sips on a glass as he stands by himself along the dining room wall.  I make my way to the back porch.

The wind blows lightly, heavy enough that when I try to light a smoke; it blows out a few times. I finally lit up and the screen doors pushes open and Michael exits, he takes my cigarette from my hand and takes a drag.  We stand there in silence, not uttering a word to each other, side by side as the moonlight embraces us.  I turn to him.
     So you know?
     "Know what?"
     About your boy and me.
     "It's cool."
     You could have told me.

"You could have told me." I smile. "He made me promise not to talk to you and I know how you like keeping your secrets." We both begin to laugh.

There are so many secrets, so much damn time.

"I wasn't that shock really, he was so protective of you."

Where's his wife?

"Divorced her, four years."

Children?

"A boy."

Him picking me up?

"Think of it as a gift."

So now you're his motherfucking pimp.

"It's hard out here for a pimp. Come on would I be that damn obvious."

Yeah! We both laugh; it is a full laugh, one that vibrates in the belly of your stomach. I love my brother and I see in him, something I miss, happiness. Michael is fulfilled.

We finished our second smoke and Simon enters our space with two drinks in hand. He hands one to me and sips on the other. Michael sort of looks around then turns quickly and enters the house. Simon sits on the steps next to me. We begin to talk and he tells me about his marriage and his divorce and shows me pictures of his little boy. I feel his arm glide around me, I do not move and he pulls me into him, the wind begins to sound like music caressing me in song, I turn to him and for the first time in almost two years I feel desire, I want to make love to him. I want to break away but I can't, I am frighten and excited at the same time. I now understood I could not run forever, I could not hide away from life. This is where it begin and maybe this where it should start again. His eyes spoke so many things, history, and hope, lost opportunity and there was that beating heart again. I lean into and I awoke.

## A New Beginning

*My Nigga, My Friend my Solider*
*I have never found myself in a place where my heart hurt
so much because I heard the pain in a voice. I wanted to
reach inside and rub and caress your heart.  Knowing
that this is not possible a nigga just wanted to be that
man, helping God carry you until you get to place where
you can once again walk on your own.  Knowing that I will
have to lean on you one day and you gain will have to
lean on me makes my heart restful because it is the first
time that I have experienced these emotions where I
can't stop lovin'/thinkin'/smilin' about you.*

*My Nigga*
*I feel you, your masculinity caresses me. Envelops me
and holds me strong.  Hold me tight.  It is in that I find my
peace and comfort.  It is the way you come strong, letting
out all that is fake and being Gabe.  Your willingness to
be vulnerable in/with me is what truly makes you a man,
not all that tough Tony bullshit (I say that with the Al
Pacino accent).  You are the man that I desired, longed
for and hoped for, the one I said would love and be down
for when he is my mine and I am his.  The nigga that I
tried so hard to make others fit into but they were unable
to fill your place because it was already destined for you.*

*My Friend*
*When I know that I need a laugh, I come to you. When
you need a shoulder I am here for you.  We will
experience life together, not just as the love of our lives
but the friends we longed for.  I want to experience life
with you not just live it.  In you I know that what I am
doing, I am bound for the mere essence of Gabe, that
your friendship is the cologne that I only have to have
one spray and it will be there for eternity.*

*My Solider*
*Stand up, stand up, I know my boi is standing there for
me, side by side riding into this battle called life together.
This love will be tested and it is up to us to leave no man
behind.  We are in a war that for a long time we fought*

I awoke with a new zest for life; I was to start work today I was actually looking forward to going to work for BROTHER, one of the new magazines targeting black men.  There were no doubt lots of challenges that awaited me and I hadn't looked forward to waking up for such a long time.  My work had begun to suffer this past year, nothing seemed that important.  I sometimes still hear Aries voice calling me in the morning, asking me if I was ready for my cup of coffee.  Today I felt his breath against my neck but I turned only to realize he still was not there, I grabbed my pillow and squeezed it to fight back yet more tears.  Death is a cruel beast, it takes more then that person, it takes part of the soul of those left behind and you just know you'll n ever get that small piece of you back, no matter how hard you pray for it.

As I walk in the office I look around the room for signs of intelligent life, I want to determine right away the flavor of the office so I can guide my way through the politics of magazines.  I had to learn quickly working for The Journal that it was a tough business and everyone is out to get the next story before anyone else. The office had the clamor of afro-centric vibe, from the colors that lined the room to the paintings on the wall. As I scanned the room I did not spot a familiar face but a deep baritone voice shook me from my focus.

"Well I'll be damned, Gabe, what's up."  I turned to face the college friend and the person who had told me about the job, Wilson Wright. We went to Northwestern together, he was a few years ahead of me but we had become friends.  He stands there smiling at me, his white teeth still glowing and his broad six-foot frame still in tack.  He had packed on a few pounds from those days and a few more age lines but not much else about him had changed.

"It's good to see you."

You too, it's been way too long.

"Did you get settled in alright?"

Yeah, Michael and his wife did most of the work.  I look at Wilson and images flash through my head, he was one who always did what felt good, no matter what the consequences. When we first met, he was up front about what he wanted and although I was still struggling with my desires, his confidence made me so sure that I was ready, even knowing that he had a girlfriend. We carried on for months but it never got weird for either of us.  Wilson bed never stayed empty, he got me through several cold months.  I could tell him anything, confide in him about everything and I never felt judged, never felt insignificant. He was a very nice looking black man, strong features, massive thighs that could pick up your body and guide you where you wanted to go which I experience on several fervent nights in college.

"Let me introduce you to a few of the fellows, we have a staff meeting in an hour and after you settle in we'll go get a bite to eat and catch up."

Cool.

"Good, then follow me. So you glad to be back to a real city, one with some character."

ATL isn't bad.

"Maybe for a visit but to live, hell naw!"

You should try it.

"We both know I'm up for anything but living in Atlanta, think I'll pass," he says with a smile.  Wilson was nice guy but he was at times distance, I don't know if this was a protective measure or what.  Before we actually hooked up, I would watch him move through one person and on to the next one.  At first I didn't understand.  The first night we met he made a play for me, I ignored the move and he offered me a ride home from a party. On the ride home, he laid it all out for me.  At first I didn't know whether to be pissed off or what but a week later we were fucking in his apartment, then we hung out and watched some TV and there was never any weirdness.  When he would see someone chatting me up, he would speak and move on, never any crazy shit.  The sex was formidable.


16

"Gabe this is Reggie, he's the politic editor, and this is my boy Gabe, just moved back from ATL.

"Welcome back," those were the first words that I ever heard from the lips of Reginald Hicks.  "I read some of your work, pretty well, you're tough as hell."

I try.  What did he mean pretty good?

"I have to go make a few phone calls, but we'll talk."

I look forward to it.  With that Reggie walked across the room, I watched him with my ears for a few seconds and when I looked up, he was looking back.  He was slightly taller than me, toned body, not an everyday gym person b any means but he was perfectly sexy.  He had short curly hair; natural His glasses were these nice frame glasses, covered his slightly bushy eyebrows and magnified his dimples on his copper cheeks.  His eyes crinkled around the edges when he smiled, and his teeth glistened to increase the attractiveness of his oversized lips.  When we shook hands I could feel his long fingers, embrace my entire body through my hand, they were beautiful hands which led to faintly hairy arms.  Everything about his seemed to be placed perfectly except his ears which stood our larger than one might expect, never taking away from his appeal, I don't think much could.  This only added to his quiet, bold presence.

The meeting went pretty well, besides being the new guy everyone seemed pretty welcoming. I had my first assignment, I was to profile one of Chicago's up and coming politicians, Jesse Johnson Jr.  The profile seemed to be more of a fluff piece.  His family was the next political dynasty and not caring for his father that much, I knew I wanted to do something more hard hitting so I knew he was not going to get the white glove treatment from me.  The managing editor and owner Eric Reynolds talked to me in his office; you could tell it was his intimidation room, to remind me that the article was no more than a profile.

"I know you have this reputation of taking the gloves off but let's just ease ourselves into this place."

If you wanted marshmallow, why hire me, why put me on this story?

"There's no doubt you're good," he said with a smile, "but you're here because an old friend said you could bring the thing we were missing."

I'll have to thank Bill for that.

"I read your piece on the serial killer and I was impressed, you really leave no prisoners, but Jesse is a community icon, well at least his father is and I'm not trying to make that family our enemy"

Then you don't want me here.  I write the truth, where the story takes me is where I follow, no holding back.

"Bill was right; you are one vicious motherfucker, fine write the story, no matter where it takes you."

Next door at the little dinner that was almost filled to capacity, we sat in the booth, Wilson and I smiling at each other. It was good to have a familiar face to look at.  It made things easier.  The food smells bad but I decide to order anyway.  The waitress, some white girl with too much make up on which still could not manage to hide her scene was impatient with me because I could not make up my mind on what to order.  The more she huffed the slower I would go, I tell her to come back in a minute, I can't stand service people who don't know how to serve  Her apron was dingy over her too tight black dress, her accent gave away her Texas roots.

"Have you decided yet sir," she asks as she approaches our table.  Finally I decide on a salad with blue cheese dressing and a cup of coffee.  She gladly takes our menus and walks toward the less than stellar kitchen.

In mind I was call her a bitch I lover at Wilson and he is staring at me with this silly grin on his face.

What?

"I was just remembering the first time we met"

Did I ever apologize for that?

"Many times."

You're stupid.  I smile at him.

"Do you think of that time in our lives?"

Yes, occasionally.

"Look at us now, how far we've come."

You married with children, how's the girls.

"Their good, Brittany is four and Carolyn is six, want to see a picture?"

Sure.  He removes his wallet to show me his pride and joy.

"It's funny, when I heard you were looking to move back home, I wasn't sure whether I should call or not, I didn't know how I would react to you."

And now?

"For now, its memories, good ones, no regrets. I love my wife and girls wouldn't do anything to jeopardize that, but sometimes, I do wonder if you would have had a different response, where we would have ended up."

Something's are better not knowing.

"Yeah, how do you tell your wife, the only man I ever loved is back in town when she doesn't even know you had sex with a man let alone once loved one." Loved? I begin to search my database for signs. I mean we had fun but in love. Wilson and I connected but the connection was more physical. Love, how did I miss that? For a brief moment I wanted to love him but the only warmth he ever gave off was between the sheets.

"You looked confused."

I am, I mean 16 years later you tell a nigga you loved him and what else is there but confusion.

"Back then, I didn't think I could love another man, not in that way. It was hard you know. You seemed so relaxed and sure about your attraction, I never was, I wanted to tell you but I figured it was just fucking, nothing more and eventually I would settle down with a female and all would be aight."

Which you did.

"Yeah, the day I fell in love with Vicky, was the same day I realized I had been in love with you. It all made sense."

Our food arrives at the table at exactly that moment; Wilson reaches over and puts his hand over mine.

"You my boy, I just thought it was time to be honest." Time had done wonders for Wilson, he had become a man. As I ate, I thought back to the last time I saw Wilson, we hadn't seen each other in about a year, he had stopped by because he heard I was leaving for ATL and wanted to wish me well. We sat around talking about what was ahead of me  I remember thinking that there was something different about him but I blew it off as my anxieties about leaving the only place I had ever known. We lay on the floor watching a college football game, Notre Dame and Michigan, I don't remember much about the game, I just remember Wilson leaning over and kissing me. This kiss had intensity to it; we rose to our knees and begin undressing one another.  Our lips met again and his mouth begins to move over my cheek, then neck and shoulders. He leant me back and begins to massage up my inner thighs with his tongue, it was not as rushed or hurried as other times, and his was purposeful. There was closeness to this encounter.  I laid there waiting for him to lift me to enter me as he had done so my times before, even after a year our bodies connected.  With a couple of slow grinds and soft and forceful thrusts he was inside me.  He pushed his way into me and once totally connected he laid on top of me, neither one of us moving.  Are you alright, he asked I shook my head yes as he lowered his lips to mine. Our tongues danced for what appeared to be hours and he begin driving into me, moving his mouth over my nipples.  He leant over and took my dick in his mouth, it stood hard and quick with each flicker of his tongue.  I felt my body open up to take more of him and he quickly lifted me up and brought me down on to him.  I wrapped my arms around him; it was a potent, striking powerful ride.  His hands on my waist guiding me, pacing our action, I could barely breathe.

  "Gabe.  Gabe, you ready.

  Yeah,

  "Where were you at?"

  Right here, I replied.  He had created that memory for me, one that I had somehow put in the back of my mind.  It's funny no matter how well you think you know a person; it's what goes unsaid that helps you really know them.  That last night I didn't pay attention to that.  The final encounter was Wilson message to me but I was too damaged to even hear or see what he was saying.

The rest of the day went without a hitch.  I met a few more people and talked about my work in Atlanta.  This place would be a nice change of pace. At the Journal everyone wanted the front page and since I was the new guy with a front page story, I was not treated warmly.   I was helping sell some papers so Bill kept me around for longer than even he thought.  Then there was Aries, his love was so powerful for me. At work I couldn't kept my sexuality private because Aries was so visible in that city. We were office gossip before I even knew what hit me.

I was home from my first day and I decide to jump in the shower.  As I step out the doorbell rings, I grab the thick white cotton towel and wrap it around my waist and make my way downstairs to the door.  When I open it, Simon stands with a goofy grin on his face; he's holding a bottle of wine.  I haven't seen him in two days.  I was surprisingly happy to see him.

Let me go put something on, make yourself comfortable.

"Don't do me on any favors; I actually like you as you are."

Just go get some glasses out of the kitchen and I'll be right back.  Since that night on Michaels' back porch I wondered if I could get to know Simon again. When we were younger it was awkward for us and the world around us had played a large part in our demise. Simon had made the first move when we were younger, this was my play.  Looking back at the way it happen, him just showing up that Sunday afternoon, my parents at a revival. Michael would not be back for a few hours, he was gone with his flavor of the week. Simon comes into the house, teasing me the way he always did.  We sat on the couch watching the Knicks and Bulls; it was before destiny was a stone throw away.

"Look how you've grown up, not that little squint that we use to pick on."

I can fuck you up.

"Watch your fucking mouth; I'll still kick your ass."

Kiss my ass, bitch.  He grabbed me and we begin to wrestle, he was of course stronger than me and he ended up on top of me.  I struggled for a minute, and then my body just stopped.  I was laying on my living room with the body of the boy I had longed for crushing me  I looked up at him our breathing was heavy and I don't remember who lips reached up to touch first. But the other one made no effort to move. He lifted me and removed my shorts and my fruit of the looms.  He begin to suck on my neck, then on my chest, he never went below my waist and I begin to lick o him like I seen in Michaels porn.  He grabbed the top of my head and pushed my head onto his lower self.  I opened my mouth and he pushed up inside of it.  He shot in my mouth quick.  He rolled me over and we kissed again.  I felt his hand engulf m dick, I wanted his mouth there but I was afraid to even mention it to him.  He jacked me off and I felt him get hard on my thigh.

We kissed and grinded but I think we both were afraid to go any further.  Afterwards we sat up against the couch.

"This won't happen again." Two days later it did and we progressed, we explored each other and learned a lot. A few times later, he gave me head. I don't know when it became love making for me but somewhere between him sucking my dick and him fucking me, I fell in love with him. He quickly let me know that he was just getting his rocks off. He brought some girl to our house and made out with her. It broke my heart, but I was determined not to let him see that. Cassandra Wilson, blaring from my living room, brought me back to the present; I quickly button my shirt and made my way to see what would be rekindled.

As I made my way down the stairs, I stop for a moment to watch Simon; he was staring out the window. I want to know what he was thinking. What am I doing? Was he nervous, I know am. He stands in the window, staring out into the streets, the light shines back on him. Dressed in a pair of blue dress pants, with a light blue dress shirt, with a multicolored tie, his face was faultless; looking at him I am underdressed in my white t-shirt and blue shorts. He turns to me and gives me the most exquisite smile, showing all his pearly whites.
     "I like the previous outfit a lot better," he says still glowing. I walk down the rest of the stairs and he approaches me. We meet and he grabs me and pulls me into his arms. I am swept away with rapid emotions, I feel my temperature rising and I am transported back to the first moment where he touched me. This was real, so familiar. I stand there looking into his eyes, something has awakened, I haven't felt this vividly, this had no connection to the past, and it was deeper. I was frightened, it was a sharp pain that was rushing to my heart, and this was a dangerous place.
     I'm glad you came by.
     "Me too." He takes my hand and leads me to the couch, hands me a glass of wine as I sat as he makes his way beside me.
     "So how was your first day at work?"
     Good. I think I'm glad to be home.
     "That makes two of us. I hope I can make your return better."
     You're off to a good start, I tell him as I ease into his chest. He puts his arm around me. I can stay this way forever. We talk about the office and he tells me about his day. This was

becoming comfortable so quickly as often as I look at him, it's no wonder he doesn't get nervous but he keeps touching my head and he continues caressing my shoulder. He looks at me with such grace.  It was as if my life had been some novel and he was now writing the ending.  With every touch I felt safer.  I don't know if he is what I need but he is who I want.

Cassandra continues to play on the I-Pod; we drink the entire bottle of wine.  For the first time in over a year, I know tonight I will not fall apart.  I ask him about his ex-wife.

"Her name is Sara, I met her about a year after you left town."

So what went wrong?

"It was wrong.  I did love her but what I felt for her was more out of fear of what I felt for you.  I wanted to convince myself of who I was and I wasn't fair to her."

So what made you leave?

"I decided to become a man.  For so long I had denied who I was out of fear, that I decided it was time to be a man and just end it.  Don't get me wrong it was hard and Sara just couldn't accept it and she kept pulling me back, she played on my fears, losing my son.  A year ago, I just stopped, I had to."

You did become a man.

"Until now, I only had my son to look forward to," he says as he looks me in the eyes. He was trying to read my eyes, but no one could for so long, he reads something because he kisses me and I kiss back.  I climb onto his lap, he takes my glass and sits it down and then his glass, wrapping his arms around me, he pulls me closer and closer, I feel as if I am falling into him. Then I stop.

"What's wrong?"

Nothing.  Nothing was wrong, I was a little frighten, not because I feel guilt but because I feel no guilt   Where is the guilt I lean back into him and I kiss him, his tongue and mine get to know each other, every inch and section of our mouths  I stand up and lead him to the bedroom.

After he falls asleep, I walk to the window and watch a lone woman come up the street her tight leather jacket, with the collar up, protecting her neck from the nights cold wind.  She looks back every so often as though she is frightened that someone was following her.  A police car rolls up the street, she watches the police car whizzing by, shakes her head in disbelief.  Then it was empty, silent and no one.  The stillness grows powerful, soon the resonant sound of alarm clocks would begin to sound and the houses would evacuate the morning people.  A thought crosses my head, a scene would now occur between a boy and a girl in some room.  They would be making love as I had spent the night doing.  Was it love?  I don't know, neither would they, it just sounds nicer to call it that.  I head back to the comfort of my bed.

The next morning I wake up with his man beside me.  He is still sound asleep, it is only six in the morning  I sit on the bed and learn the sight of his body, which I had explored to well by touch and taste during the night.  He has a tiny scar right under his belly button.  His legs are slightly hairy but powerful.  It is hard to imagine this man had his legs wrapped around me doing the night and who my legs had wrapped around.  His arms so puissant and statuesque limbs that held me and blown me into such enormous heights lay stretched out on my bed he is peaceful. He has light fuzz that covers his jaw.  I lay back down onto his arms; he immediately wraps them around me. I can't fall back to sleep.  I have too much energy to sleep.  My arms seem to move on its own between his legs, grabbing for it, finding it and I feel it come alive in my hands.  I look up at him and his eyes slowly open.  I meet them with a kiss and reach over into my nightstand for condom.  I tear it open and put it on him as he watches gently caressing my head.  He lowers his lips to the top of my head, kisses my neck, his tongue baths my head and shoulder blades so profoundly. His head lowers; I know where he is with each kiss.  He rolls me over and spreads my legs with his knees and raises my body as his grandness enters me.  It was here, the passion, the sex, but not love, but I was sure that would return, it had too.  After years of dining on love, you cannot settle for anything less.  I had loved him once and I feel that I can love him once again.  We rock back and forth; my mind went from the future for the present was good.

We shower together, not saying much but just touching each other.  After we dress, I watch him.  I wonder what is on his mind. He turns to me and pulls me down on top of him, looks lovingly in my eyes.

"Don't hurt me." Those words don't hurt me. I know what he means; he is going to try not to hurt me. He reads my soul because the previous night with ever thrust, I had repeated them silently into his soul. I lean up to him and kiss him and I say what I know he wants to hear.

I won't. My reply would be his and he would never try to hurt me but people hurt people all the time that they love, whether you are gay or straight, lover or family, people always get hurt in the end.

As I walk in the office and settle n my desk, a young mail clerk passes by. His name is Will, I find out as he stops and talks with that goofy thuggish air around him as he works his way around the room. Will walks from desk to desk before he arrives at mine, his short hair acknowledging the scruffiness of his face and yellow tint of his skin. His eyes merely sunken into his face, with protruding red lips that bleed sensuality as his small Dumbo ears encase his perfectly shaped his eyebrows. His cheeks make his youth more visible. He wears a USC tie with a black pants and white shit. He hands me a letter, I take it, and he reminds me of my college friend Wesley. Wesley was hard and insisted he was straight. I never fought him on that. I guess that is why when he I finally got to stick my dick in him it made the pleasure feel that more intense, but like so many things, I outgrew Wesley. I could not help but to smile at his twenty year old boy, God I hated when people referred to me as boy when I was his age but really I was just a boy.

Will stops and turns around and I begin to calculate how quick I could get him into bed. I decide to let this moment pass but I do put him on my memory rolodex for future reference. I open the letter it was from Bill. Inside were best wishes and it helps start my day off right. I pick up the phone and begin to make my calls, how tedious this seems to me. No one wants to talk at least not about the Congressman. About an hour into one of my man dead ends, Wilson appears and begins to tell me about his interview that he had set up with Larry Fishburne. He was all excited and wants to know my plans for the evening; I politely decline because I had plans with Simon, and so I gave him a rain check.

It was hours later and still hadn't gotten any further on my research. I sit at my desk, watch the people pass by, not knowing exactly what to do.  I decide enough is enough and grab my things and head out the door.  On my drive back into Hyde Park, I decide to stop at Medici and grab some dinner.  It was one of my favorite places to hang out in college.  I sit at the table which is carved with names and wait for the unfriendly service to finally make her way over to me.  I was having dinner alone.  I was never the one to mind eating alone but tonight it was made more obvious because I was the lone person at a table where everyone else was either in groups or coupled. This is where it hits me; I wasn't ready for a relationship, not with Simon, not with anyone. I knew when I laid down with Simone he took it for more. Was I a bad person for leading him on, was this the payback for the pain he had cause me.

As I begin to munch on my spinach pizza, I start to think about dream I had a few nights before I left for Chicago.  It was my brother, my father and myself, we were in a burning building, trapped with no was to escape.  My father falls to his knees and begins to pray.  A bright light appeared and an angel appears and he begins to talk to my father in a corner. This was not your typical angel.  He was dressed like Harlem in the nineteen forties.  His wings came out of his jacket.  His brown hair laid back with his brown and white plaid suit, patent leather shoes and a halo for a hat.  He and my father keep looking over at Michael and me.  We were slowing losing our energy because the fire was coming through the door, as I slowly begin to pass out I could hear the conversation as if they moved beside me.
    "I can only save two of you," The angel says.
    "I'll pay you fro the extra body", my father says.
    "Listen, make your choice," the angel says firmly to my father.  My father walks over to me, looks me directly in the eyes and said without even a hint of pain in his voice.
    "Sorry kid, he wouldn't accept the money, we'll see you on the other side."  With this the angel lifts my brother and father out of the window and lowers then to the ground.  When I tried to leap out the window, the angel takes hold of my arm.
    Let me at least see if I can survive if I jump, I tell the angel.
    "Hey, he put on a good show, but the old man paid me to make sure you didn't get out.  I felt myself wanting to cry, but no tears would come.  I just sat silently and begin to sing but no words came out of my mouth, only music.  It flowed in the

loveliest and saddest melodies I have ever heard.  The angel begins to rise out of the building as the flames begin to engulf me.  I awoke at this point but the dream seemed so real, it still haunts me.  The sad part is I can't be sure my father would not want me to perish.

After I pay my bill, I push through the door, the nice Chicago air hits me in the face like a huge gush of wind, rips my inside. The trees teeter back and forth as quickly as a fat kid sits on one side of a teeter tot that throws a skinny kid off. A woman passes me and smiles as I stand and watch her as I wonder where she is headed in this weather. I enter my car, the wind seems to calm down, the trees stop their hurried movement and wind seems to take peace.  I drive home and was there in five minutes.

As I leave my car, I see Simon walking towards me.  His face was not only lit from the streetlights but something else makes his face glow.  I could not help but smile.  He reaches for my briefcase and puts his arm around me and plants a kiss on my cheek.  We enter the house, I take off my jacket and he removes his own. I walk with a purpose to my I-pod, and play Lena Horne. She begins to sing *I wish I had known you when were seventeen*, I turn to see his face lit with the very essence of sex, or was it love.   The same face I had known so many times when I brought him into my bed late at night while everyone else slept.
  "Can I have this dance," he asks as I walk into his arms and we begin to move with every sound that came from the speakers. He holds me tight and I selfishly let him, knowing where this is headed, hoping it would go there.  Every ounce of my being wants it to go there quickly. *What would we have known about love*, Lean sang as my eyes close and my body unlocks, *I'm glad I never met you, I'm glad I never met you when we were young*, she sang.  I had known him known Simon for a long time but I had never met him, until now.

The room seems to disappear from me.  I was inside some holding cell, holding on to this man as if everything that was dear depended on this very moment, in many ways it did, I was dependent on this very moment.  I know if I can just let go and relax, I would be able to move on from a meaningless death to begin my life over again.  Simon was rescuing my soul from the pit of blame and anger but it isn't a lone rescue mission, I am

doing the same to him.  We don't say a word but the room is
filled with conversation.  It echoes off the walls, bounces off the
ceiling and crashes inside our eardrums.  We hear it and anyone
who could see us could hear it, it was loud.

The next morning I awake and Simon sits in the bed, he watches
me.  I reach up to him and kiss him with deep severity.
        "You sleep like some angel, I couldn't wake you."
        Well thanks, I'm glad I could give you pleasure even in
my sleep.  We both laugh.
        "You don't have a clue what I am feeling for you, do
you?"
        What you could find another fourteen year old to wait
your dick with?
        "When we were younger…"
        …When we were fucking.
        "Yes, then," he says uncomfortably. "I never considered
you more than another a piece of ass.
        Well I hope I was a good piece of ass, that's what really
counts.
        "Stop it", he says as he smiles a leans in and touches my
lips. "After I was married to Sara, I thought again and again
about you for the first time in years and I couldn't understand
why.  It was strange I had forced you from my mind, I had to."
        Listen we don't need to go over the past or try to make it
more then it was.  We were young and naïve and I thought I
loved you.
        "Did you really love me?" I don't know how to answer this.
I truly did love him, even though I was young and was years
away from understanding love.  What I felt for him was different
from ever boy I laid down with after him.  I gave everything I
knew how to at that age.  He was my life for that period of my life
and after it ended my life went spiraling out of control.  I look at
him and answer the only way I know how.
        Yes, I loved you, the only way I knew how.  We're getting
to know each other again, just this time it feels like there is hope.
        "The first night we were together, I planned it; I knew who
would be there.  The reason I kept thinking about you when I
was with Sara was because I realized that I had felt strongly
about one other person and that was you."
        What am I to say to that?

"Nothing", he says as he gets on top of me.  He pushes my ass on the bed and I struggle with him.  We are frolicsome in our play.  For the first time I was not focused on what he was doing to me but what I was doing to him.  The day passes into night without incident.  We order food and lay in each other's arms.  We are relaxed, we have dexterity.

## WHEN YOU LOVE SOMEBODY!

Three months pass and I am starting to feel close to normal.  I had just come back from seeing a really good flick that starred Laurence Fishburne. The film was dark and creepy but can the man get any sexier, his co-star Nate Parker was nothing to blink at either, you had to just stare at this brother. I am also feeling good because I caught a break in the bribery case against Jesse Jr. I finally have a source on record admitting that he paid the congressman seventy five grand for his vote on an environmental issue facing Colorado.  I also was about to get a chance to meet Nate Parker and that had me really excited, sure it was fluff but I looked at this at chance to show the intelligent side of a young brother.

I am headed to Michael and Kim's for dinner and Simon was coming along with me, this would be our first family dinner as a couple. The more I try to slow things down with him, the more they sped up. I'm looking forward to a good home cooked meal since I had no talent in the kitchen and Simon couldn't turn on a stove. In the past month I have spent every dinner with Simon except on Fridays when he had his son.  We hadn't made that move yet, it didn't seem the right time for such an event. Simon is anxious about moving in that direction but like my momma use to say, if it meant to be then nothing will ever be able to stand in the way. I am in love again, which feels amazing. I never thought I would feel this way but two years later, I love a man and his name is not Aries.

The traffic is heavy as I drive down Lake Shore drive.  The DJ from V103 tells some silly joke about Whitney and Bobby.  We all knew the deal going into this relationship.  The boy had enough children to start a football team and Whitney kept on dragging her ass with him, can you say Mr. Provider. Who can blame her; every diva from Chaka Khan to Aretha has a phase that they must endure to get to the status of icon. It was Whitney's turn and I'll be damn if she didn't go along with her drama. The wind is blowing and the breeze is giving me that extra dose of life I need to get over all the hard work of today.  A song from the Romeo and Juliet soundtrack plays, I believe it is Desiree.  It is a beautiful song, it was that way when I first heard it and remains so today. Cause I'm kissing you, I'm kissing you.  Touch me deep, touch me true, give in me forever, cause I'm kissing you. Tears roll down my cheek, it wasn't from sadness.  It was tears of memories, tears of joy.  Damn, I have to let go of this pain.

I pull off of Lake Shore Drive and move my way down sixty seventh, a block west of Jeffery into Michael's driveway and get out of my car.  I walk up to the door.  I spot Simons car, so I know he's here. I walk up to the door but before I can ring a bell Kim swings pen the door.  She has the most peculiar look on her face.  I give her a hug.
Is anything wrong, I ask?
"No," she says but you can tell she doesn't mean it.  I look over her shoulders and I see Simon whose warm glow is only accentuated by a gloomy smile.  I walk to him and give him a small lip lock, his lack of reaction tells me something is going on.
What's wrong?
"It's your parents."
What about them?  My relationship with my parents was nothing more than non-existent.  I had not seen them since I return to Chicago. I start to worry that something terrible had happen and I would never get to tell them how much I loved them and how I wish they could love me for me. Before Simone could answer I hear footsteps and look up and my parents walk into the room, down the stairs behind Michael.  Once they see me they stop in their tracks and stare at me, then move their heated glance to Michael.
"What is he doing here," my mother asks with such bitterness. Michael looks at me and then at them as if he has just stolen from her purse on Sunday morning.
"I asked him to come to dinner," he responds.
"Then you shouldn't have invited us," my father hurls not at him but directly at me. It hurt the same way it did years ago when he told me I was no longer part of his family.
"This has to end," Michael muffles out. "I can't take this any longer." He seems to be at a point of whimpering if from nothing else but pure exhaustion. Simon moves close to me, he must feel my knees beginning to lose their strength. I dare not reach for his touch.  My parents like him; they always have, if they knew of us what they would think of him now.  I have carried their anger and disappointment for years; no one should have to carry such a burden.

At the table there is not much conversation, we slowly ingest our meal in comfortable tranquility. Then it was broken, this soon proves not to be a good thing. My mother asks Simon about Sara.  We all look at each other and leave him out there dangling like a piece of meat in between their teeth.

'We aren't together any longer," he says.

"I know that, I just thought I heard someone say you were working it out," my mother says not knowing how spiteful and cruel those words actually were. Simon looks at me and I stare back at him.  Michael never stops eating and Kim was ready to jump out of her chair.

"Well," my mother asks, "are you trying to work it out or not?"

"The Lord believes that once you make the commitment of marriage then nothing should ever stand in the way of keeping it," my father says.

"I'm seeing someone else; we've moved on," Simon releases, "Our divorce has been final for a while now." Simon looks at me and smiles.  All my insides yell don't do it, don't tell them.  My heart was being a little more selfish, I knew it would devour them in guilt to find out that we were together, that I had corrupted their other son at least that is what they would think. As much as I loved them I hated them for not loving me, for not accepting me.  No matter what I did with my life I would always be that faggot that God hated so they must hate.

"Who are you seeing," my mother asks.

"Simon, no," Michael blurts out, "this is not the time."

"What's the big secret," my mother asks, "just tell me." He hesitates for a second, not knowing whether to continue or just let it go unsaid.

"I'm seeing your son, Mrs. Richards, I'm in love with Gabe, Simon replies.  With these words I felt a sense of excitement.  My parents had once said that some sick man must have done this to me, that man was Simon Bennett.

"My God," my father uttered, "it's not enough that you destroy your own life, you have to corrupt everyone around you. You are ruining this man's life, he has a wife and child for Christ sake."

"No, don't blame him, your son was the first person I have ever truly loved, I thank God for him," Simon says.

"You've perverted him too.  You people are sick, my mother lashed out at me.

"Stop it, that's enough," Michael says.  I can not move or respond.  I am paralyzed with both anger and fear. I heard the words begin to come out of my mouth but I could not control them.

Ruin his life, what a joke.  I didn't ruin his life and I sure in the hell didn't ruin yours.  I am so sick of being your punching bag, you self-righteous hypocrites. You sit there and act like who I am is the worst abomination on the earth.  For years I have put up with your shit, why, because I loved you and I prayed one day that you would just fucking love me.  Every chance you got you tried to destroy me, make me feel like I was worthless.  Am I any worse than you daddy, who sleeps with woman after woman, pretending you giving them spiritual guidance, am I any worse than my mother who can't put down that bottle of booze to go to church on Sunday sober. I am still that little boy who you gave birth to and all I ever wanted was your love, not your judgment. I had to run away from this city once because you told me I was nothing to you; I'm not running this time.

"Gabe, stop," Michael yells to me.

No, Michael, not this time.  I don't want to do this anymore. I won't let them destroy my happiness or soul this time, it took too long for it breathe again.  To think I felt guilt about not being the son you wanted, well guess what, I'm the son you got and just for the record you have not been for one day the parents I wanted or deserved. So there it is, out there.  We're all just damn disappointing.


I leave Michaels and drive back to my house. I can't go inside.  I told Simon I wanted to be alone but that is far from the truth.  I begin to walk through Hyde Park, a walk I use to do quite often. It was dark out and I had been walking for a while.  I was brought back to reality by a bunch of loud college students with a smell of liquor that poured from their body like cheap cologne. Maybe it was cheap cologne because I couldn't depend on my senses at this point. The street was nearly empty, except for the occasional white teeth that passed without saying a word.  I was beginning to get tired and my stomach was growling.  A police officer passed me and gives me the look.  Tonight had been a night of anger and pain at this moment I could kill my father.  I needed a drink.  A car pulls up beside me a man who appeared to be close to my age pulls up next to me rolls down his window and peers out.

    "You need a ride", he asks, his smile, which was hauntingly eerie, shows me he has more in mind.  I kindly decline and he rolls up his window and continues his slow drive of pursuit. The last time I was here was the summer after my senior year in high school. It was the day of my seventeenth birthday party and everyone was there, neighbor's friends and all except Simon.  He didn't show up.  That night after everything was calm down, I was sitting on the porch talking to my cousin EJ and he came up and asks if he can holla at me for a minute. So we took a walk down the street.

    Where have you been?

    "Busy."

    What's wrong with you?

    "Nothing, now."

    Man, you acting like someone just died.

    "It's done dude."

    What are you talking about?

    "All that faggot shit, I can't be doing that shit, and you had me thinking that shit cool but it ain't."

    I had you, what the fuck is wrong with you?

    "You faggot!  Nigga just stay the fuck away from me."

    You know what fuck you nigga, I say to him as I push his head with my finger and walk away.  I was angry and I couldn't go home.  I was weeded up and drunk and he came there and said all that shit to me. I walked and ended up here.

I must have seemed out of place.  Football jersey, black shorts, not thinking about where I was going or what I was doing.  I just needed to get away.  For over two years, I had given that nigga not only my body but my soul and he not only stomped on my heart, he set fire to it, I remember thinking and feeling that anger. I can pulls up beside me, a handsome face appears, and he had to be in thirties.

    "You're a little young to be out here this late."

    Really.

    "Let me give you a ride."

    Naw, I'm kewl.

    "Let me give you a ride." I stop for a minute and looked at him; he didn't give a damn about how old I was.

    Fine.  So I hop into the car.

"Want to go to my place?" I look at him and smile, and then look over at him.

I'm not that young, pull over there.

We park and he places his caterpillar fingers on my thigh and slides it up my leg, he unzips me and my dick springs out and he leans in and takes me in his mouth. I could hear his hunger in ever moan that escapes his lips. I just sat there and let this man devour me. I wished that I was someone where else, anywhere but my thoughts are brought back to this place as I feel the cum begin to rise from my dick. My thoughts were gone for a brief moment; I had almost forgotten that my first love had broken my heart.

He took me to get something to eat afterwards then dropped me off at home. When I got out his car Simone and Michael were sitting on the porch. When Michael saw me he got up and walked up the stairs and Simon jumped up in front of me as I begin to walk up the stairs.

"Where the hell have you been, your mother was worried," he said in the most irate tone, "we looked everywhere, your father is pissed."

Why are you here, I asked in the most spiteful tone I could muster up, not wanting him to see how hurt I was at this moment.

"Who was that guy?"

You don't want to know, I said knowing this would only give him more interest.

"Who was he?"

None of your damn business. Simon grabs me by my jersey and we look into each other's eyes and for the first time, I saw his pain and he saw mine. He lets go and walks down the stairs out the gate, down the street toward his house. I went inside and to be grounded by my parents. After that day Simon and I barely said more then a sentence to each other and I begin my journey of protecting my heart but not my body.

**Family Ties**

Forty Seventh Avenue was quiet, mostly lit up from light from the closed stores and the street lamps.  Now and again someone would pass but hardly ever a couple.  At one corner stood about four or five young boys, maybe in their twenties, drinking and talking trash to each other.  As I passed they stopped and took a look then continued their conversation.  I hardly looked up from my walk, when a hand grabs my shoulder, my heart raced as I turned quickly to see Will standing there.
"Hey you didn't say hello."
I didn't see you.
"You walked right pass me."
I have a lot on my mind.
"Anything I can help with?"
Naw thanks.  Why are you standing out here?
"Just hanging with my boys. Where you headed?"
Home.  Don't you live near 99th?
"Yeah, I get the bus."
We're not that far from my house, come with me, I'll give you a ride.
"You don't have to do that."
I know, are you coming or not?
"Give me a second."  He jogs back to his boys, they shake and he takes his place beside me and we head to my house. We talk about work and about his experiences at DePaul. I must admit he was tempting, he was twenty, sexy swagger short buzzed hair, and lean body all fitting together so perfectly. His light brown eyes made his face glow every time he smiled. His ass was perfectly round which was made that more attractive by the way he walks.  His walk was firm and laid back, I could fuck him but not tonight.

As we pull up on ninety third and Paxson, Will jumps out of the car and leans back in.
"Thanks for the ride."
No problem.
"We should hang out sometimes; you're pretty cool for an old man."
Shut the fuck up, I say smiling.
"My girl is throwing me a party tomorrow night for the twenty first, you should stop by."

Where?

"You have paper and pen?"

Naw.

"Then I'll call you and let you know, oh you can bring someone if you want."

Thanks.

"Peace." He slams the car door and I peel off as he jogs up the porch stairs into his house and I head to my home to sleep. I need to relax.

The following morning the talk in the office was on my article about Congressman Johnson. He tried to double talk me but I had enough of present and former staffers who had knowledge of deals he made and I was ready to take him down. There was denial by the congressman and I didn't have him on tape but I did have one of the business ventures, who had been caught up in the sting by the FBI admit to paying him off to vote against environmental legislation on Compo Mountain. Now my story wasn't as exciting of catching Donna Rice on Gary Harts' lap or Clinton and the intern scandal but it would give me a few more headlines and a few television shows to sit on to discuss the case.

"So I hear you're taking over the Fishburne interview," Reggie says interrupting me from my thoughts.

Yeah, Eric thinks I should do some easier stuff.

"Hey don't knock the fluff, the fluff gets people to read your articles."

Now what does that say about our readers?

"You mean the people who pay our salary?"

Yeah, those people. Don't get me wrong, I'm of fan of Larry Fishburne but do I have to be the one who does this interview.

"Just have fun with it."

I will. Reggie turns and walks to his desk and I continue to look over my notes.

At home, I was getting dress for Will's party, when the doorbell rings. I stop in the middle of my shave and make my way through the maze of discarded clothes to my front door. As I open it Simon stands with his baseball cap tuned backwards, hands in his pocket, looking down at me with those piercing gray eyes. I smile and give him a hug. We stand in the doorway for few moments wrapped in each other's arms.  I look up at him and he places his lips onto mine, I am taken back by the hunger he has for me that I almost choke on his affection.

"You going somewhere?"

To Will's birthday party, you want to go?

"Not really dressed for a party.  I tried to call you last night."

I needed to be alone for a while.

"Are you alright?"

My parents can only hurt me for so long.

"I tried to explain to them, I wanted them to understand."

Don't waste your breath; they don't want to hear that.

"I care about you."

I know why you don't get a shirt from my closet and we head to this party.

"I just want to be with you, not really up for a party."

We won't stay long; I just want to stop by. Something was wrong with him. I know he was hurt last night but this couldn't be it, he had known how they felt for a long time.

"Let's get me a shirt."

We'll stay an hour or so, and then we'll come back here and talk.


On the ride over, Simon wasn't doing much talking.  He held on my hand as often as he could on our drive over.  His arm remained around me, as disconcerting as this was; I know deep inside me that he needs to be this close.  We pull up in front of the house Will had left on my machine; it was already in full swing.  People on the porch, music blares from the door.  I begin to open the car door but Simon doesn't move, I close the door and look over at him.

What's wrong?

"I didn't mean for this to happen."

For what to happen?

To love you like this.

I care about you too.  His tone was ominous and that worried me.

"Do you love me," he asks with direct intent that only he knew the answer to but I felt that I should have known.  I sat there for a moment trying to figure out my answer. I had loved him once but he had not loved me. If I am honest I would realize

that I did not love him the way he meant.  My heart was still
fragile. I was again falling in love with him our souls were
connecting to him piece by piece.  He did not own it completely
and frankly I'm not sure that he ever would.

Yes, I love you.

"Really?"

What more do you want me to say, I love you Simon, my
heart in some ways always, has always and will always belong to
you.

"Do you want to hang with me and my son tomorrow?"

You want me to?

"I don't want you to do it for me, I want you to do it
because you want to be apart of our lives."

I would be honored to share that part of your life.

"I told him about you."

What did you tell him?

"I told him that you and I were special friends and that I
wanted him to meet you."

How did that go?

"Fine, he told Sara he was going to meet you, She was a
little more honest with him, I don't know if it was out of spite but
he knows about you."  I was frightened for him, I knew there was
more to this story but this was a big step it was no longer about
sharing a bed or a night, it was sharing a lifetime. I lean over and
kiss him and get a glimpse of his soul but all I can see is pain.
We got out of the car and walk up the front porch and enter the
house.  The living room was filled with bodies, moving to the
sounds of Jay-Z. As we move through the bodies twist and melt
together like a dish that isn't quite ready. Girls hang onto boys
and boys fondle them like lost treasure.  Groups of girls fill
corners, where they point and talk about everyone as they pass.
A group of guys fill the back wall with drinks in their hands,
looking like frighten school boys, afraid to approach the ladies in
the room. A full figured, too hot to touch woman stands on the
back wall, surrounded by another group of men, all deciding,
more of waiting, to see who would be the lucky guy for the
evening.  As Simon and I enter and look around, we recognize
no one and no one recognizes us.  Simon, in his blue jeans and
the navy blue shirt he borrowed, we have an aura of being out of
place.  I just want to find an empty space and fill it.

I survey the room looking for Will and finally spot him as he leaves a room that was filled with shapeless smoke that disappears behind a closing door.  He locates me and smiles and makes his way across the room of momentarily vacant minds.  He sticks out his hand and I introduce Simon.  He seems for a moment taken back and immediately he goes into casual talk that is much lower than any conversation that we have ever had.  He guides us to makeshift bar and the guy in loud red shirt and smile that appears bigger than the rest of his face fixes us both a jack and coke.  Will excuses himself and Simon and I make our way to the back porch.

I pull out a cigarette and smoke while Simon looks at me with disapproving eyes.  He takes the cigarette from my lips and tosses it and pulls me close to him.
  What?
  "He has a crush on you."
  Who, Will?
  "No the Maytag repair man, yes of course Will,"
  He does not.
  "Tell yourself that if you want."
  You have nothing to worry about baby, I'm all yours.  He leans down and kisses me as the back door opens and he releases me.  Two girls exit and begin to talk to us, we fabric interest and they soon realize that they are wasting their time and make their way back inside.
  "You want another drink?"
  Sure.
  "I'll be right back," he says and enters the house, the door opens and Will comes out as I light another cigarette.
  "Let me have one."
  Here you go.
  "Are you having a good time?"
  It's cool.
  "I'm glad you came."
  I didn't see anyone else from work.
  "I didn't invite anyone else. How long have you been seeing him?"
  A few months but we've known each other since we were teenagers.
  "So it's serious?"

It appears that way.  I was getting turned on by this man and the bulge in my pants was not letting me hide it.  It was only harmless flirting.

Where is your girlfriend?

"She's around here somewhere but I don't want to talk about her."

Then what do you want to talk about?

"I have a few things in mind but I guess that'll have to wait."  Will turns and walks back inside.

I stand on the back porch and think about my life, all that has happened in the last fifteen twenty years. I use to think that I would never be happy, I couldn't be happy that was my destiny. I hated myself for so long. I ran to Atlanta to escape my life only to begin living my life. Before I met Aries, I had seen men go through relationships like bottled water.  I hate to admit this but I want what my parents had, that long lasting love.  I thought I had found it with Aries and for ten years it felt so right. If I had written it, our lives couldn't have been any better.  It wasn't a perfect relationship, we had our struggles and there was a period where I thought it was over but I couldn't let go of him, maybe, just maybe if I had, he would still be alive.  A tear rolls down my cheek and Simon pulls up beside me, he hands me my drink, wipes away my tear and without saying a word he pulls me to him.  I look at him as he stares into space, he turns to me and I relent and my head falls on his shoulder.

I love you.

"I love you too.

I wake up and Simon is still asleep.  He looks so restless even as he sleeps.  I walk and turn on the radio and Lena Horne belts out.  The high Gods above looked down and laughed at our love and say how tirade it's grown.  I sit in the big chair in the corner. Simon sleeps and I watch him, I have woken up almost every morning since we have gotten together just to watch him sleep. Simon was winning the battle of our hearts. He was so strong but at times so vulnerable which made everything about him so much greater.  I reach inside one of my top dresser draws and pull out a letter from Aries.

*If I could*

*If I could start my journey over again, I'd no doubt hold you closer.  I'd give more kisses with whispers of love abound.*

*If I could*

*I'd memorize everything you ever said to me, I'd meditate and storing it in my heart positively.  I'd listen to the wisdom and apply it; I'd listen to the music of your voice as people do as a symphony or at the tune of birds singing.*

*If I could*

*My love, my friend, my nigga, my solider and my baby, I'd find you sooner so I could love you longer, better and truer.*

*If I could*

*Love Aries*

I walk to the mirror on the bedroom wall and stare at myself, my entire five foot ten frame, my short curly hair that made my forehead just a little pronounced.  My eyebrows which so many have accused me of shaping.  My semi wide noise leaning out from my face.  My clear brown eyes surrounded underneath by the same bags that accompanied every male in my families' eyes, my ears, and small.  My small mustache shaped onto my upper lip with my chin covered by the very carefully cut goatee.  I hadn't been blessed with the same round lips as Michael and my father, no I have been given the lips of my mothers' ancestors.  I look there at myself standing in my suit of birth, I though damn I need a gym.  I wasn't fat but a tone I did need. I lowered my hand to my dick and remembered masturbating when I was younger and I would stop and think is God watching me do this but instead of stopping my intensity grew with every stroke.

"Can I play too?'  I look over to see a radiant man sitting sideways on the bed, I walk toward him, when I reach the side of the bed he pulls me down and kisses my stomach.  I look down at him and he looks up smiling.

"You didn't answer my question."

Anything you want.  I reach inside the nightstand and grab a condom, he lays back on the bed as I rip open the package with my mouth and roll into his dick.  It throbs with every touch, as every inch rolls down onto it, it seems to swell larger.  I climb on top of him and once again we dissipate into another.

Later that afternoon, we stop by and pick up Simon's son, Brian. He is the spitting image of his father as he opens the front door. His face lights up with excitement and exhilaration as he sees Simon.  This ten year old was so full of life. He's dressed in blue jeans and a Bulls jersey as he holds onto the neck of the man who was his entire world.  We enter the house, I look around and see pictures of Brian at various ages and pictures of Simon and Brian, and then I see Simon's wedding picture.  It suddenly feels like I am intruding and that I didn't belong here.  I want to escape, to run as quickly as possible out of the door.  Once Simon puts Brian down he looks at me as if to study me.  Simon introduces us and he seems to try to figure out what I want from his father maybe just maybe that is my thoughts.  Simon asks about his mother and suddenly she appears in the doorway without a pleasant look.  Her pictures do her no justice; she is a strikingly exquisite woman even in her jeans and flannel shirt. Her dark hair flows in waves down her head. Her pug nose eased into the center of her face seems to guide you to her painted lips that are impeccable.  Her dark eyes are mesmerizing and inescapable.  I could she why Simon had fallen for her, why he would love her.

She is graceful as she walks across the room, I reach my hand out, and she ignores it and hugs Simon and looks at me almost as her son had just seconds earlier but there is bitterness in her glare. I feel Simon's body tense up, he has no idea what to do. He had thought to be prepared for this moment but he was wrong.

"Daddy I want to show you my new game," Brian says as he tugs at his sleeve.  Simon looks at me and I force a smile.

"Go ahead, get his jacket and I'll keep Gabriel company", Sara says, the words coils off her lips like a rattle snake waits to devour its prey. I want to scream, No, don't leave me but before I can muster up the courage, he is gone.

"Would you like something to drink?"
No, thanks, I'm fine.
"I guess I should be happy to finally meet you."
Same here.
"All Simon can do is talk about you, but then again you are Michael's baby brother."
Yeah we've known each other for a while.
"Yes, I know.  Sort of like having the invisible elephant in the room that finally appears."  What I was to say to that, any response would seem quite inappropriate.
"He thinks you're the one, he thinks he loves you."
You don't think he does.
"No, I don't, but then I'm not Simon."
He's a good guy.
"I use to think so, but then he brought you here, the first man, so I guess that means something."
I guess.
"I wouldn't get too attached, he always comes back."  She continues to talk but her words become distance.
I'm not here to cause trouble, maybe I should wait in the car.
"He'll never be happy with you or any other man; I gave him something that you will never be able to give."
I don't doubt that but I'm not trying to interfere with that.
"Don't worry you can't," she says with absolute hatred in her voice coated with pure politeness, a tone that I had only from my parents.  Simon enters with Brian and we fled the house.

At the park, I watch Simon push Brian on the swing.  I wonder am I destroying a family.  I shouldn't even ask myself that kind of question.  How was I to blame if Simon had decided to end that part of his life.  It had happened before I was anywhere near him.  Am I to give up on love so Sara could live a fantasy that somehow Simon would come to his senses, after all I was his first love. Brian races to the slide and Simon comes over and sits next to me.
"So what did she say to you?"
Nothing.
"It's Sara, I'm sure she said something."
Why did you want me to go there?
"I don't know, maybe I was being selfish, I wanted her to understand that this time was different."

She won't let you go.

"She doesn't have a choice."

Everyone has a choice, it's what they choose to do with it is what counts. He takes my hand and moves it to his mouth and kisses it. I want to reach over and hold him and never let go. I was allowing myself to let him in completely but something was nagging inside me, it was confusion. Brian played with the other children and we sat in silence watching, now and again taking glances at each other.

I think back to when I was six, I was sitting on my father's favorite chair and my father comes in and I quickly jump up, my brother enter and sit on the floor next to me. My mother comes into the living room wiping her hands on the dish towel, she sits on the couch. My father reaches over in the drawer of the end table and removes his bible and begins to read.

"Blessed is the man that walked not in the counsel of the ungodly, nor standeth in the way for sinners, nor sitteth in the seat of the scornful. But his delight is in the law of the Lord." I sat there soon making my way onto my stomach with my hands holding my head high so I could hear every word he would say to me. He would ask me if I wanted to hear another one and I would of course reply yes and he would turn quickly, looking for another one to read. He would always close with my favorite Psalms. Psalms ninety five.

"O come let us sing unto the Lord," he would read as I sat entranced in my spot. "Let us make a joyful noise to the rock our salvation, Let us come before his presence with thanksgiving and make a joyful noise unto him with Psalms." After he finished he would lift me onto his shoulder and carry me into my bedroom and I would sleep so peacefully knowing that I was loved, never knowing that the love would be conditional. I realized it when I was twelve and my father would condemn homosexuals through his pulpit and I realized it was me he was condemning. "Man shall not lie with man as he does with woman that is what the bible teaches us. I remember him praying for this boy who could be no more than fourteen because his mother said he had the homosexual spirit, which I later learned she found him engaged in sex with a neighborhood boy. The boy just stood there humiliated in front of the entire congregation, with his head bowed and tears formed in the corner of his eyes as my father prayed for him and the church members cried out "help him lord", "save him Jesus".  I wanted to help him, I wanted to take away his pain, I wanted to cry out Daddy no, I'm like him don't do this but most of all, I wanted to hide.  No one helped him or saved him and for years that imaged haunted me, until I finally let my father know that I too was what he called "possessed with a pervasion demon".

I'm nineteen, dancing at the Clubhouse.  I am having a nice time; people are coming in tossing leaflets in the garbage and talking about the people standing outside passing them out.  I had known my father and his congregation had begun a campaign against sin and the homosexual was the sin dejour.  One of the tracts landed on the floor and I saw the familiar name that lit the sky every night as I entered Gods house as a child.  I was frozen with fear.  I could have stayed in they would not be there all night but the image of that boy that was engrained in my head became to throb on my present memory, I walked right out the door, passing the crowd trying to get in and looking directly into the eyes of women and men that I had known for years and right into my father who looked as if I was a stranger to him, there nothing but uncontrollable silence.  Wilson grabbed my arm and guided me to the car.  I sat there and stared out the car in complete silence.

When I arrived home, my father was waiting and begin to call me every name and pervert he could think of without needing to repent in the morning.  He told me we needed to pray he came and grab my hands and begin to pull me to my knees and I pulled away.  I don't know how I had the courage and strength.  My father begins to weep and I begin to cry, not for this moment but the tears of the boy I had left suffer in silence.  Then my father stopped and his expression changed and then I was on the floor, blood flowing from my nose and I heard my father.

"You're dead to me, get out."  His words ripped up my chest and all the joy seemed to vanish at that point.  I had loved this man and he had claimed to profess his love to me, now he was using his fist and words to beat me. I kept waiting for my mother to rush and save me, because I was her baby boy, I wanted my brother to come in and protect me but neither happened, neither was going to save me, I was alone. I ran out of the house, covering my face.  I ran as fast as my legs would take me.  I was slowly dying inside, my body; my spirit was all at once falling apart.  With every stride I was losing a piece of myself, as if my flesh was being torn from the bones. I was frighten, but nothing was more scary then my sadness.  I approached Michaels' apartment and relieved the occurrence with him.  He held me but I was motionless, almost numb, until a single tear dropped splashing against my cheek, then a few more then several and my eyes closed from the weariness of the day.

Those are the memories I awoke with.  It had been a week since I had met Sara, yet I had thought about her every day.  Every night I went to sleep in Simons' arms wondering if this was fair to him, to Brian but also to me.  Every morning I woke up pondering my life, my choices, and my love for Simon.  We had years of choices that was affecting our present situation, yet it felt so good to have him here, next to me, touching me, laughing with me and loving me. This morning was somehow different.  It felt different.  It was quieter but louder. Then I heard his voice, Aries voice, not out loud but it was his voice.

> *As I sit here on this blessed morning of 2:20 am, I can't stop the overflow of Gabe on the brain.  It is these affections of him that shower and sprinkle him with more desire, more longing, more just him, day by day.  As I sit here feeling like a school kid in love for the very first time, and so in love am I wanting to be all the man that he needs, to love him, to hold him, to comfort him, to listen, impartially, not judging, always down, always understanding, but above all, praying for the presence of the Lord to keep him in perfect peace, perfect health, and no doubt, all other spirits that come to encourage and minister to his spirit at the level of his needs and more. As I sit here, so full of intimate yearnings for Gabe, I only will love him with increase for the rest of his days.  He is me and I am him, I love you.*

Aries was a love like no other.  I thought I would never love again, her I am two years later and I have fallen in love again. He would be happy.  I am drawn out from my memories by a ringing of the phone.
     Hello.
     "Gabriel?"

Yes, who is this?

"This is Sara." The hush falls on both sides of the phones, how in the hell did she get my phone number.

What can I do for you, Simon isn't here.

"Yes, I know, I need to talk to you, can we meet?"

I don't think that would be a good idea.

"It's about Simon."

I'm sure, but I think you made it very clear what your feelings are.

"If you care anything about him, I mean really care, and then you'll meet me at MoJava's on 55th in an hour." She hung up the phone before I could answer. I won't go I thought to myself but who was I kidding. I couldn't be more curious about this meeting than anything else. I went into the bedroom and throw on some jeans and a t-shirt. I thought about calling Simon, to let him know what was about to happen but I decided against it. I didn't want this to turn out badly for him.

When I pull in front of the only black owned coffee house in Hyde Park, I sit in my car and watch the colorless faces pass me with little or no expression. The wrinkle old lady crosses the street, slowing down traffic with every wobble but she manages to stumble pass my car in a matter of minutes. I try to imagine what is going to happen inside, but I can't this is a new circumstance for me. I had before try to ignore an intruder into my relationship and it cost me dearly, this had to be handled head on. I open my car door and make my way out and into the coffee shop.

As I enter, the smell of freshly brewed coffee ravishes my nostrils as I am greeted with a smile by the cashier. I quickly search the room but could not locate Sara; she would be late for her own party. I look through the glass display case and order a sandwich and a medium soy latte with an extra shot of espresso. I hand the lady with the coco skin and short brown hair a ten dollar bill leaving the change behind, making my way to a table on the upper landing. Me'Shell Ndegeocello is playing in the background as I take a seat. I recognize the song as Stay from Peace Beyond Passion CD. *I must admit the forbidden always aroused my temptations, Oh baby, come on just let me,* Me'Shell sang. *I want you, I'm thinking about you, I can't get you off my mind, oh, you turn me on, do you think about me, do you feel the way I do*, roll through the place.

I look up from my latte as Sara makes her way up the stairs, never removing her eyes from me and the man almost tripping over a chair cannot take his eyes off of her.  She sits down and looks away briefly to place her purse in the empty seat. She returns her gaze to me and smiles malevolently.

"This doesn't have to be so bad."

Excuse me.

"I'm not here to argue points with you, I'm only here to prepare you, it is the least I could do since no one had the decency to prepare me for losing Simon."

I'm not losing him.

"First mistake, never underestimate a fathers' love for his child. So here it is. I told Simon he had forty eight hours to make a choice, either his son or you.  I made it very clear that in no circumstances can he have both."  I look at this one with so much anger but more than that pity.  She was in so much pain and I realize that Simon was a huge cause of it.

Don't do this.

"He'll tell you tonight most likely.  If you love him, you'll make it easy and just accept it.  That's all." With that she stands up.

Stop, I blurt out. She turns to look at me.

Sit down, it's my turn.  She lowers her purse back in the chair and avoids eye contact.

You think by destroying Simon and me, it'll bring him back to you, I will let him go because I wouldn't want any man to feel that pain, if that's what he wants but he won't go back to you because for him it would be to truly understand how much you despise him.

"You think you have all the answers, who the hell do you think you are.  He is my husband, the father of my child and there is no way I'm going to let a faggot walk in and take him from me."

Your husband, the father of your child, if you don't realize is a faggot.

"Go to hell!"  With that she turns and calmly walks down the stairs and out of the door.

Eight months with Simon and here I am sipping on a Heineken and listening to Me'Shell.  *Tell me I'm the only one, I want to marry you, tell me I'm the only one*, she sings, *so give me what I want, tell me I'm the only one, I want to marry you, tell me I'm the only one, satisfy me for free.*  Nothing was for free.  No matter how it appears at the time, you have to pay for everything.  Life is a very expensive gamble and maybe I made the wrong gamble and I was going to lose.  The song ends and another begins to play and there is a knock at the door.

As Simon enters and sits on the couch, still in his jacket.  I stand by the door, watching him.  He is in so much pain and it pours out across my living room from every crevice of his body.  He begins to weep.  I walk to him and wrap my arms around him. I had never thought I would have a future with him but things had changed; now I could think of anything more.

"I think maybe we should just break this off."

Why, knowing full well why.

"I've met someone else", he says avoiding my eyes.

Don't lie to me.

"It's true."

Simon, I love you, I at least deserve the truth.  He stands and walks to the window, looking out.  The room was so subdued that I could hear his tears hit his cheek.  They echo so loudly that the eardrums to my soul feel like they are being burst with every drop. He turns to me and looks me in the soul as the pain rises in his eyes.

"Sara told me if I continue to see you, I couldn't see my son."

What did you tell her?

"She was crazy, but she's right no judge would give me any custody knowing about us.  I know you can't understand but this is my fault, I'm to blame."

Do what you have to.  I turn to walk away and he comes behind me and grabs me pulling me into his chest.

"She's hurting, before you came back, I tried to move on, I saw a few other men but I was scared and I always went back, because she was safe.  I knew she would be there and I wouldn't be alone."

So you used her?

"No, yes. I wanted to break free from it. I told her to go on with her life, find someone else but she didn't and I couldn't.  You

50

gave me that strengthen to move on, to let her go, but she didn't she was determined to make our family work but she knew something was different with you."

Simon.

"Let me finish, last night I went to visit Brian and after he went to sleep, she kissed me and I told her it wasn't going to happen. I told her that I love you.  Her face filled with rage, I had never said that about another man before and she told me it was either you or my son.  I can't lose my son.

Just stop, alright just stop.  I want to feel contempt for him but I can't.  I want at this very moment not to love him but I am so in love with this man.  I want someone to wake me up from this excruciating dream but most of all I just want to pull him close to me and hold him and love him one last time.

"I'm sorry, I, just, can't lose him, not my son."

Then you'd better go, just turn around and walk out of the door.  He looks at me and the pain is there, visible.

"I love you."

Just go before, I can't say that to you.

"I love you, the day I married her, I was in love with you. I have wanted you for so long.  If I even had thought for a minute we could have this, I would have…"

Just go.  Don't make this any harder.  If you stay, you'll hate yourself and eventually you'll end of hating me.  Just leave.

"Maybe if we give this awhile, she'll calm down and we…"

No, just get the fuck out, I can't let either one of us do anything to hurt each other.  Simon walks to me and pulls me in his arms and we kiss, as Me'Shell blares out, *when we make love I feel it so deeply, when we make love I cry.  When you kiss me my lips burn with fear, for your love that crowns me, crucifies me, when we make love, when we make love, when we make love, I feel you so deeply.*

Pain is a word that many people use but very few understand.  I can destroy your soul to such an extent that no amount of time, no measure of love will be able to heal you. At least you believe and feel that way.  I have had that pain.  It seems to be a constant in my life, never subsiding; it only grows with each passing day.  My life is a series of pain.  No matter how I try to stop the recorder in my head from adding to the painful moments, it never stops burning the image onto my recorder, it never shuts off; life has never given me enough. Instead it because more precise, more pronounced, more visual and more ravenousness.

For weeks I walk around in a daze, not knowing what to say or do.  Simon stops by a week after we said our goodbyes but I can't allow him to stay long.  It is too painful.  My world is uncontrollable at this moment.  Every time I see a place or notice something he has left behind it is only a reminder of another memory I will not ever get to experience with him.  Michael and Kim try to comfort me but they cannot help with the feelings that I have yet to come to understand.  I was angry at Sara for using her child as a weapon but somehow the reward she receives will only be bitter.  I want to blame Simon but his gift was utter emptiness and I did not wish him that.  With no one to blame, where would my anger go. I just want to anger to vanish.  I lie in bed at night, sometimes tears fill my bed like an ocean other nights it is emptiness is my company.

It has almost been a year since my return, my birthday is near. Michael invites me to his house to celebrate but I decline, I will watch it pass as quickly as it has come. I sit in my house and listen to a Rufus CD, when there is a knock at my door.  I open the door to find Will standing in brown leather jacket, baggy jeans and a Michigan jersey.
	"I was in the neighborhood, I just wanted to stop by and say happy birthday," he says with a grin on his face, the same one I vividly remember from the night of his party.
	Come in.
	"Why are you at home?"
	Where else would I be.
	"Out celebrating."
	Ah, young one, when you get as old as I am, you don't celebrate the simple things.
	"You should, when you get as old as you, you might not have so many more."
	All right, fuck you.
	"I'm kidding."
	You want a beer?
	"Sure."  I walk into the kitchen and remove a Heineken from the fridge. When I return Will has made himself at home, removing his jacket and hanging it on the closet door.  He riffles

through my cd collection.  I smile a slight grin, I welcomed the company.

Here's your beer.  He takes the beer and sits on the couch and watches me.

"So how's Sam?"

Simon. He's fine.  Why are you here?

"I wanted to see you, isn't it obvious."

Not really, besides you see me all the time.

"That's different. You're not going to make this easy are you?"

Not on your life. You have a girlfriend.

"I'm not looking for a girlfriend."

Just a fuck. He stands and walks to the cd collection.

"Now who's making assumptions, besides, I don't have a girlfriend."

All right, so we can be clear…

"…I'm looking to just have a good time, no matter what happens."  I look at him, he smiles. I think I've just been punked by a twenty one year old.  I head into the kitchen and grab a couple more beers.

A few hours later we are in the shower, when the phone rings, I jump out and head into the bedroom to answer it.

Hello.

"Michael told me to call you and let you know we are about fifteen minutes away."

Can you stop by tomorrow.

"No, we're not taking no for an answer, so open the door, besides we have keys."  I hang up the phone and I quickly remember the soaped up tight body that waits for me, so I rejoin Will.  He turns to me as I enter and grabs a steady hold of my dick and I instantly grow to full mast.

We can't, my brother and his wife are on their way.

"Should I go?"

Naw, you don't have too, unless you feel weird.  I'll make sure they're in and out.

"Sounds good to me," he says pulling me by my waist into him.  I giggle, yes damn it, I giggled.  I turn the water to cold.

Cool off, why don't you, I say while make my way to put on some clothes.  I was going to kill Michael for this little stunt. I hear the doorbell so I make my way down the stairs as I open the door, Simon stands with a box, with a red ribbon on it.  He greets me with a smile and his hazel eyes. I want to reach out to him.

"Happy birthday," he says, looking at me so full of love.

Simon, thanks, what are you doing here?

"You didn't think I would forget did you?"

Michael is on his way and I don't think it would be a good idea if you stay here.

"I won't stay long, just until you open the gift."

Simon, please, I thought we decided it was too hard to do this.

"It's your birthday, just open the box." I walk inside, Simon enters and I begin to quickly un-wrap the package, I was praying deep inside that Will would stay up the stairs but I knew with each second that was unlikely.  Inside was a picture of Simon, Brian and myself, I look at him and he smiles.

"I know things are difficult for us but this is how I will always picture us."  He moves to me and we hug, it was so ardent, so deep that when I felt his body grow stiff, I knew Will was there.  He moves way and I turn to see Will at the top of the stairs.

"I'll wait upstairs," Will says and turns and leaves as quickly as he appeared.  I turn back to Simon and his head is down.

"I guess I should have called. I should go."

Simon wait.

"I knew you moved on but damn, with that boy, what you into changing shitty diapers now."

That's not fair, you made a choice.

"I had no choice."

Does that make it easier, go ahead.

"So what now you want to get them young and mold them."

Naw, I just decided if I was get with confused as niggas, I was gonna to get them young and at least enjoy the fucking.

"Don't you think I would be here if I could?  My God, he's a child."

No, he isn't.

"I guess, I really didn't know you."

Don't say that shit to me.  I'll be understanding of your choices but don't you walk your ass in here and think I'm goin' to apologize for mine.  Do I love you, yes, but that isn't enough, so I don't need you to walk in here and get self-righteous with me.

"It's just, it, it hurts.

Yes, I know.  I think you should go.  Simon opens the door and walk out into the windy night.  It wasn't pain I felt, it was relief.  It was gone, it was finished, there was nothing more, what we had was closed.

I go up the stairs and Will sits on the bed, he stands when I enter and I can feel him staring at me but I can't look at him.

"I'll go."

Why?

"I don't want to intrude."

You're not, I want you here.

"You sure?"

Yes, positive.  I promise no more ex's making their way by.

"You sure."

Come on, we need to get downstairs and clean up a little before my brother gets here.  We head down stairs to get rid of the beer bottles, and put the couches correctly on the sofa and hope this night would resettle into what had start promising at the beginning of the night.

## An Unforeseen Presence

Two weeks have passed since the night Will and I hooked up. We have seen each other almost every other night and it feels great to not be worrying about where this is headed or where it might lead.  Tonight we have decided to go dancing. As we walk through the doors, I realize how much I hate the overcrowded, packed sweaty bodied clubs but here I am.  People are staring at us, sizing us up.  Hard body boys are walking, acting indifferent to anyone and everyone around them and older guys, my age are guzzling down drinks as if to do is the last day alcohol will be made. For some this might be a stone thrown from heaven, for me it was the epitome of regret.

We make our way to the bar and order two rum and cokes.  We turn to look at the dance floor and it is semi-crowded and the floor was made like an old deserted street in the ghetto, full of potholes and pitfalls. The music was all right but it could have been better.  Men and boys alike walk past us mostly eyeing Will. There is something in his face that is more relaxed then I have seen him before. In his white tank top and black button shirt that is open hanging promiscuously from his body. His toned body is only emphasized by the clothes that he wears. I am immediately turned on by him and I pull him closer to me, whisper in his ear for him to follow me.

I make my way to the dance floor, with Will right behind me.  As I reach the dance floor I turn to face him and he looks at me in my eyes. I can feel his breathe on my chin and I desire this man even more.  He smiles as we dance and my lower body gives away my desire to him. This is desire that is unfathomed at any imaginable level and my body cannot hide any other signal to him.

      "Let's get out of here", he says and I agree, after all two hours had been quite enough.  We make our way out of the club and into the car.  On the ride home I can feel both mine and Will's anticipation.

As we enter the apartment and the door closes behind us, he pushes me against the wall and attacks me and I surrender myself to him.  His touch, the sweat, the breathing, the desire does not overwhelm me, instead I embrace it. I give myself to

Will.  He accepts my gift without hesitation and he lives up to all expectations that I have.  His appetite is entirely fulfilling is both. I had been the leader, the guide, his teacher and tonight he wants to show all that he has learned and I am eager to partake in his exam. After several hours of work, he falls asleep.

I stand naked at my window, looking out into the night at the park across from my place of residency. The lights from the street light bounce vibrantly off of the park cars and make strange shadows onto the street.  Every so often a car passes by disturbing the silence of the night. Will does not lie still in the bed as the constant movement makes me turn to look at him. He looks up at me and over his shoulder is a picture of Aries.  It took all my strength to refocus onto him and not reach past him and grab the picture. It was quiet and the wind was the only sound that was available to us.  Will stares at me and his light brown eyes center on me as he tries to read my head.

    "Come back to bed", he requests in such a manner that I cannot help but grant him his wish. I walk over to him and stare down at him.  Two weeks and the secrecy at work had developed into winks and nods that had not seemed to bother either one of us. I understood it was sex and I believe he knew the same. As I lay down next to him, he raises and kisses me.

    "I spend more time with you then I do my girl", he says, looking as if I should be pleased.

    Does that bother you?

    "Nope", he replies, "I just didn't think that I would be into this thing."

    This thing.

    "Yeah, these things, messing with another nigga, like this."

    You want to stop?

    "That's not what I'm saying."

    What are you saying?

    "I want to be in you." He kisses me again and rises over me, reaches into the draw and removes a condom.  I take it out of his hand and open it and begin to roll it down his hard dick. I grab the bottle of lube by the table and apply it to his dick as, he raises my hips upward and places the head at my opening and pushes his way inside me. I slide down onto him and he gasps and begins a steady pace. The sweat pours from our union and spills onto the white sheets and our hands intertwine. The various shades of our skin tone blend together as one wet mass of electrifying passion.  His pace picks up and I feel his dick throb inside me as his moans grow louder, I feel him explode.

As we lay in bed, I turn my body to the window and he slides up behind me.  His body is connected, resting on me and after a few minutes I hear his sound of peace and I am to follow shortly. It is as if someone has just infiltrated my body and now released me. I pull his arm and wrap his arm closer into me and he moves body yet closer without a word. I close my eyes and begin my wait for the distance sound of an alarm to reopen them.

At work the next day, I am finishing my article on Congressman Johnson and the office is quiet.  It seems the Christmas season has kept most people out of the office.  I was still typing when Reggie enters and sits at his desk.  I try not to look at him but my eyes cannot stay away from him.  He has a very intense look on his face and we do not make contact.  After he makes a phone call, he walks directly toward me, holding an envelope.
        "We're having a New Year's party; I hope you can come, bring a date to whatever." I look up at him and watch the manner he is speaking.  I take the envelope and place it on my desk.
        Thanks man, I'll be there.
        "It'll be a good time."
        Alright, cool.  He turns and goes back to his desk as if I no longer exist in his selective world.  I return to editing my article.

Wilson enters about an hour later and hands me a small package.
        "So you have plans for tonight."
        None I can't get out of.
        "Well my wife can't go to the Bears fundraiser, you want to tag along."
        Hell yeah.  I can do that.
        "Meet me at the front of Museum of Contemporary Art at seven. It's formal."
        I'll dust off the tux, and see you there. I pick up the phone to call Will and cancel our plans for the evening.  There was no answer and I decide not to leave a message.  I grab my bag and leave, nodding my head at Reggie as I exit.

As I ride down the LSD, the high wind blows, the water over onto the top of the land slowly pilfering the street.  The trees sway recklessly seems to tip almost as if they were touching their toes. A jogger dressed in blue sweats and headphones seems to have escaped inside the sounds that blare inside his head, not once turning toward the street. Here I am stuck in my car with the rest of the motorist praying for a steady pace to pick up.  I turn to my car to the local radio station to enjoy the rest of ride home. I notice a woman in the car next me and am immediately fascinated by her. Her red tint modern beehive hairdo sways from the slight breeze from her open window.  She might have been attractive if she had hidden her beauty in all the atrocities of contemporary beauty.  I turn up the radio as Luther Vandross begin to blare out of the radio. *Didn't know till today that you would love for me to say, all the things I fear, though you don't know they're real*, he sings as I finally my way pass the cars and onto Lake Park Avenue.

I pull up in front of my house and exit my car with haste.  The traffic had put me behind schedule so I had to hurry.  This place has started to feel like home and not some strangers' house I had borrowed for the weekend.  I hang up my jacket and embark on my task of preparing for the evening.  As I pass my phone the blinking light catch my eye, so I stop and press play.

"Listen Gabe, man, this is Will, man I don't think it's a good idea for us to kick anymore.  You cool but things just got too complicated.  I hope we still boys.  It was followed by silence. Will was a nice guy but I never wanted complicated, had enough of that to last a life time.  I want fun and he had been fun.  I rush up stairs and get dress for the evening's events.

As I made my way down Michigan Avenue, from the overpriced parking garage, I spot Wilson standing in his tuxedo.  He looks ever so dashing.  It is something about seeing a black man dressed elegantly that drives me absolutely wild. His frame seems somehow built for that exact tux.  He spots me and smiles.

"Nice clean up", he says as he pats my shoulder.  We walk quickly up to the MCA and enter. As we enter the big room, I marvel at the structure and detail of the place. The chandeliers hanging from the ceiling are unique in their design; they are crystal with chains of silver balls that hang around the light adding to the grandeur of the room.  The room is filled with well-dressed people who marvel at their own importance.  Tables are meticulous lined with exquisite white linen napkins and blue and white settings. An eighties retro band plays while a few brave souls dance with offbeat enthusiasm. I search the room after grabbing a drink, not knowing what I was looking for but then I saw him, surrounded by an army of white guys, who acted like teenage groupies at a concert. He stood with a smile frozen on his face.  I had seen him play for the first time at Northwestern in my senior year of college.  He had broken big ten freshman receiving records. He was called the most gifted wide receiver since Jerry Rice his first year out of Chicago.  Four years later he was injured and this off season he had been traded back home to Chicago. At twenty eight he still had amazing speed, even more amazing hands and agility that most rookies pray for. I think our eyes just locked but he quickly turns back to the crowd. I can't take my eyes off of him, then he looks up and this time he smiles. I walk to the crowd.

Shaun, they need you in the back to talk to the mayor, I say.

"Oh, all right, thanks.  If you'll excuse me fellas." He walks away turns when he gets to the end of the room, raises his drink and keeps walking. I stand near the bar having yet another drink. I feel someone move beside me.  I turn to see this six feet four rugged man, chin so jagged and yet so perfect, his ear slightly off but somehow balanced by the remainder of his face. I am not sure if I should look at him or turn away so I continue to look at his caramel skin glisten exuding his strengthen, toughness, roughness and powerful elegance.

"Thanks for giving me a breather, it was driving me crazy listening to all their sport antidotes."

No problem, if you'll excuse me.  As I turn to leave, I think what the hell am I doing, I have one of the premier athletes right here, next to me and I was turning to leave, he grabs me by my bicep.

"I'm Shaun Sharpe."

I know who you are.

"Yeah, I guess you do, so you're at an advantage."

Gabriel Richards.

"Can I get you a drink?"

I have one, but thanks.

"I guess you do, I don't know why all of sudden I'm nervous."

I think I am the one who should be nervous.

"What is it that you do?"

I write for Conurbation.

"I read it."

You have a subscription?

"No."

You should get one.

"You can sign me up."

Tell your agent to give me a call, now if you'll excuse me, I need to go speak with someone.  It was nice meeting you.

"The pleasure was mine." With a huge grin, I make my way across the room to Wilson and enter the conversation he is already engaged in. I turn back to where Shaun had been and he was not there, I scan the room and he is standing talking right in my front vision, he smiles.  The rest of the evening we didn't say two words to each other but our conversation remained continuous.

I was tired so I say my goodbyes to Wilson and head toward my car.

"Gabe," I turn to see the face of Shaun as he jogs as he jogs to me.

Hey Shaun.

"Can I give you a ride home?"

I drove, but thanks.

"Good, then you can give me a ride." I look at him as an unforced smile crosses my face.  He has assumed so much about me already, I guess my attraction was obvious.  It might have been the drool that kept running from my lips as I talk to him.

What can't you big time athletes afford cars or is the child support.

"No child, so no support. Are you going to give me a ride or what?"

Come on.

We make our way down the street to the Michigan street parking garage.  We stand at the elevator for what seems like twenty minutes but could only be two. He does most of the talking. I try to avoid staring at him, but every now and again, I cannot help myself.  We are joined by others who appear to be from the same event, they talk to him, pat him on his back, and I just stand and listen.  Occasionally he looks over his shoulder and gives me a wink but he keeps the couples engaged in conversation. As we enter the elevator he stands right in from me, he backs to my body and for some reason I think of a clothing ad he was in.  He was shirtless cowboy, pecs perfectly ripped, cowboy had scarcely over his shaved head, pants tight with no belt with a saddle over his right shoulder, as he looks away from the camera leaning against a wooden fence.

As the elevators open and the people exit, he says his goodbyes and leans back onto me and the doors close, he turns.
   "I thought they would never leave."
   Admit it you like the attention.
   "I think we all like the attention but there is sometimes when you want some alone time." The elevator opens and we exit. We walk in silence to the car.  Once we are inside, I turn to him.
   Where to?
   "Can we get something to eat?"
   Sure, where?
   "Someplace we can just chill out."  I start my car and hit a little late night diner on the north side.

Sitting across the table from Shaun, I watch him demolish a plate of pasta and buttered bread.  The room was lit lightly; I could barely make out the faces at the other tables.  Watching him smile occasionally as he eats forced a smile on my face.  The gray table cloth, matches the gray sparkle in his eyes.  I slowly sip on a glass of red wine as he took gulps of his mineral water. I was a huge sports fan and I am not sure if it is the football player that had my juices running or if it was the man, more likely it was the combination of both. I continue to watch him, not really knowing what to say or what to expect. Occasionally he will tap his finger on the side of his glass.  What did he want from me, better yet what could I give him that he could not so easily get from some other place. Aries made me feel free, safe and I knew that he wanted to spend the rest of his life with me, because he made that very clear.  Shaun was physically perfection.  Most people would trade their own inner beauty just for a moment inside Shaun's perfection. Thankfully I had grown out of that but I still had insecure moments about my body.

Shaun wipes his mouth and took a deep swallow from his glass
of water; I run my fork into my last ounce of Alfredo.  As I look up
he was watching me, following my fork to my mouth.

What?
"Nothing."
Can I ask you a question?
"Sure."
What are we doing here?
"Eating, what does it look like?"
That's not quite what I meant.
"I just needed a break, to relax and you seemed cool."
All right.
"Do you have a girl friend?"
 Is that a trick question?
"Boyfriend?"
Another trick question.
"Answer one of them."

How about both, no. I watch him and want to ask him why
I seem cool.  I just want to take him to bed right now. I didn't
want to be the one with my ass hanging out. We sit and talk
about his career and my life. I drive him home and drop him in
front of his building.  We exchange numbers and I tell him I
would call him in the next couple of days.  He says he would
keep in touch and I drive off. I make my onto my block and
Shaun is taking over my mind. As I get out my car, I look around
at the quietness of the houses. At the house two doors down a
couple sits.  A young fair skin man and his darker complexion
mate sits, she is between his legs with her arms wrapped around
his legs, as he leans back.  A small portable radio sits next to
them playing a nice soft tune as they appear vanished in another
world where no one else exists. The light from the dimming
street lights illuminate their bodies, it was a beautiful sight I think
to myself as I turn the key and enter my domain.

I am awakening to the sharp ringing of the telephone.  I reach
over and pick up the receiver trying not to sound like a fire
breathing monster rudely uplifted in its liar.

Hello?
"This is your morning wakeup call", the voice rings in my
ear.  I immediately recognize it as a smile slips across my face.
I see you are up early.
"It's almost nine."

Yes I just went to sleep four hours ago.

"Sorry, I just wanted to talk to you before you left for work this morning."

I'm glad you called.

"I know you have to go, so I'll get the point of this call."

I thought this was the point.

"Sort of, I have to go to Detroit for the Christmas game and was wondering if we could have dinner before I leave?"

Like a date.

"Um, yeah, I guess, if you're not into that…"

No, I mean yes, dinner would be good.

"My place seven o'clock, is that good."

Perfect.

"I promise you a good meal and some good conversation."

All right.

"Then I'll see you then, I'll text over my address to your cell phone."

Cool, I'll talk to you later then.

"Most definitely." After hanging up my phone I jump out of my bed and run to the shower, tingling with excitement.

The water hits my face like a stinging bee, going from slightly cold to exceptionally hot. It splashes onto my body making its way onto all the areas of my body that had been previously without moisture. The twinkling feeling coming from inside me was bringing all of senses to life, making me aware of every small fraction of my body. It was working its self through the openings between my toes encouraging them to wiggle with delight, crashing onto my shoulder blades and running down the spine of my back with severe purpose. I reach for the bottle of body wash and lather up my towel until white suds appear, placing it on my small head with vigorousness of motion. I slap the towel on my chest and underarms, then up and down my legs, up and down inside of my thighs where my movements became even more precise. I rinse myself with the water and repeat my moments one last time. A shower can be a fun event if you work it the right way.

The events of the day seem to fall as slow as newly spiked molasses trees getting to their last drop. I try to contrive some concern of my daily activities but there is really no sign of interest anywhere to be found. Whether I would admit it or not Shaun had taken my breath away. Maybe I was being shallow because the brother was fine but the conversation was interesting and I like the fact that he was pursuing me and this makes me feel really good. After the recent events with Simon, I really didn't want to feel the emotions he had left me with. Somewhere over the breakup with Simon I had once again shut my heart off or at least turned it to low vibrate. I know it had been one night of food and conversation but Shaun seems so sure of what he wants. That stability felt good to me. I am not going to jump into a relationship quickly, but jumping in his bed well we'll just have to see.

Eric enters the office room and stops to talk to Reggie but I felt him staring a hole in the back of my head.  He eventually makes his way to me and asks to see me in his office.  I follow him into his office and his solemn gaze tells me whatever it is, it is not good news. I take a seat at one of the chairs in front of his desk and he stands and looks at me.

"Will called off his engagement."

I'm sorry to hear that.

"He and my niece were supposed to get married this June but he says he needs to work some things out."

I'm sure it'll be fine.

"No, I don't think so, Katie thinks he has been seeing someone else, says he's been distance."

I'm sure she has nothing to worry about.

"That's why I brought you here, you and he were friendly, you too talked."

Yes, we were not quite what I would call friends, but we did converse when were both here.

"Did he ever mention anyone?'

I can't say he did.

"If you hear anything."

I'll let you know.  With that I make my way from his office. Damn his niece, how did I miss that.  I really didn't care. I didn't want to know any more than necessary about Will. He came into my life when I needed to feel a warm body, when I needed to be wanted and I gave him freedom to be.  Now we would have to wait and to see what he actually decided to become.

## Repeat

Michigan Avenue was quiet at this time of night. The last reminder of the busy afternoon was leaving the area.  A police officer stands talking to a man in front of a vacant coffee shop were the only sign of life that I could see.  Peaceful as it was I was not there integrated into the peace. I had become even more uptight and nervous as my dinner with Shaun grew nearer. It seems crazy for me to go to his apartment.  The light turned green as I made a sharp right turn into the building where Shaun lived.  The parking attendant let me through, without any questions, he informs me my fee had already been taken care of and he gives me a number space to park.  I tip him a ten dollar bill, he gives me a stub and I park my car and proceed to the elevator. I push twenty eight and a lady enters right before the door closes and she appears to be a little hesitant. The elevator ride is a quick one and as the door opens for her first and I go up an additional fourteen floors. As the door opens on twenty eight, my heart begins to beat so fast, so violently I think it will explode at any moment.

The elevator doors opens and I walk off, looking for the door number but there was only one door.  I knock on the door.  A few seconds past and the door opens, Shaun stands in a pair of black slacks and white dress shirt open slightly enough to reveal the top of his pecs. I smile at his smile and enter his domain. He takes my jacket from me and invites me to have a seat.  He walks into the kitchen; I could smell the scents of the simmering meat, spaghetti and the aroma of garlic bread. He returns with two glasses of wine and hands one to me, I thank him and walk to the window to admire his view.  The beauty of the Chicago Skyline over takes me.  He walks up and stands behind me.
      "It's the reason I took the place, beautiful isn't it", he says. I turn to him.
            Yes it is.
            "I mean the view."
            Me too, I say.  I look up into his sparkling eyes.  He begins to talk and I responded but my mind was swimming.  I look around the room; one side is filled with trophies and a super bowl ring in a glass case.  The apartment is full of energy and I begin to wonder who had taken the time to decorate it for him. He excuses himself and moves into the kitchen.  I take a seat on

the couch.  He returns into the dining area and sits down a bowl and tray at an already set table.

"More wine," he asks as I move so he can fill my glass.  I sit at the table, he sits across from me. He says grace and fixes my plate.  I watch as his rugged hands fill my plate and sit it down in front of me.  He fixes his own and then we begin to eat. This is all too familiar but somehow I was holding back.  We eat, with rare conversation between us.  We both had talked so much on that first night.  It was if the stakes had been raised in a card game and we were waiting to see exactly which one of us were bluffing.

"Do you like jazz?"

Sure.

"I know this great little club, it's a little out of the way, and I thought we might go there after dinner."

I would love too. Somehow this seems to lighten the mood.  We begin to talk more.  He laughs at my attempts at jokes and I do the same at his.  We weren't trying to impress each other.  No forced laughter but true real, spontaneous sound.  He talks to me about his game at Detroit and he hopes that it would be a lot easier than the previous game at Dallas, which they had won with a last minute field goal.  I thought back to this morning paper that referred to him as the hero of that game because he had caught a bad pass by the quarterback to set up the last minute field goal. All day the channels kept replaying the catch.

Sauce runs down his lips, he licks them and something begins to grow inside me.  As I watch his tongue runs smoothly across them catching ever single drop that stands so thickly on his plump succulent lips.  I take a sip of my wine, and then I take a bit out of my garlic bread. I look up and find him watching me. He bows his head with a grin embarrassment.  He has been caught doing what I have been doing all night enjoying the view. The tension in the room was easy to feel, it resonated with lust.  I could fill out my spirit leave my body and meet his in midair and rub against his. I want then the spirits I want to reach out and touch him. His fingers open the top of his shirt, small beads of sweat had begun to appear and it excites me. I look into his eyes and he is watching me.

Are you hot?

"Yes, but the air conditioner is turned on."  My body screams, I have to catch my breath but instead it tightens up.  I hear a moan pass from his lips. The room seems to rock back and forth like a small ship lost on a formidable sea.  It is violent or maybe it is suggested violence. I close my eyes to let my mind refocus.  I want him to take me to his bed, I want to feel his lips on me, and I cannot let him know this.  I open my eyes and he watches me with a transfixed gleam.

"What are you thinking?"

Oh I can't tell you that.

"I can guess, it is exactly what I am thinking, I was hoping that mine were pretty transparent. I smile at him only replying yes to him.

I am so captivated by him, the way he tilts his he as I talk.  He is so interested in every word that comes from my lips.  He knows when to laugh and when to just smile.  Everything seems so perfect.  The atmosphere was just as smooth as the rest of dinner, the low light in the room, to the soft jazz that plays in the background just loud enough to add to ambiance of this ideal evening. Maybe this was just his usual motive of operation.  He would bring someone up to this place and let the view and his carefully created game and body seduce them. He did not need much to help him with his seduction; he had already won me over. Yes, I want him, I could feel my prick call out for his touch, and I could feel his lips call out for a taste. Shaun is anyone's fantasy, he was a dream and I was living inside one with him.  I see desire in his eyes; I could see his desire for me. Maybe it wouldn't last a life time but I could not count on anything to last that long, life had caught me that cruel lesson and maybe it was not quite finish with me yet.

We hurry through the rest of dinner.  I think about making my move on him but I think better of it.  I don't want to give myself away too quickly; he wouldn't be impressed, I am sure he was not unfamiliar to the idea of one night stands or first night sex. There is a tangible twinge of jealous that rises up in me at these thoughts.  I was envious of those other men who had knowledge of what I was definitely on a path to experience. More to the point of his touch, as his fingertips traced their way across my naked body, leaving unseen lines of pleasure with every stroke.

We stood at the doors of the smoky jazz join, gazing inside, sensing instead of seeing the crowded atmosphere of the room. The music was loud and lifeless.  Most of the people stood around drinking and doing nothing much of nothing.  The music is not moving in the least.  I wonder why here, did no one know him or did everyone know him.  We make our way to an empty booth near the back of the cub.  The smell of alcohol mixes with beer giving the place a dry stale smell.  The door opens and with every new entry a little life is breathed into the room.  I begin to take in the music.  The band plays reassuring everyone of what laid ahead of us.  I excuse myself and go to the bathroom, where I find a young white man leaning over the counter taking white powder up his nose.  He turns when I enter, holds his nose and smiles as he makes his way from the bathroom, looking back trying to see if he recognizes the face that has entered.  Once he decides he doesn't, he leaves. I wash my hands, and then toss some cold water on my face.  I look in the mirror, what am I doing, I think to myself.  It's terror really.  Not of him really, more myself. I have allowed myself to put to sleep all these feelings of lust after Aries and it had been so damn easy for them to reawaken, first with Simon, then Will now with Shaun. I thought Simon had put them back in their grave but here I was again, letting them reawake and not even with caution. Am I determined or just consumed with the idea of love. When I look at Shaun, he seems to look through me, inside me, as if he could see my very soul with his bountifully beautiful eyes. I could not hide myself when I am with him, it just comes out, every emotion, and every feeling he brings to the surface with each look.  I fumble with every turn with him, I feel as if I had become a school boy, in my khaki pants and white shirt and he was the head master, completely in charge, finding out every secret that I want so desperately to hide.  He stares at me and look into my eyes and I look down trying to avoid the glare of his penetrating eyes, what can I do but give in.  How can I resist the yearning that still grows inside me for him?

Returning to the table, Shaun is not alone, there a man sits with him, and from a distance their conversation looks intense.  I slow my steps; I don't want to intrude on what appears to be a deep heavily involved conversation.  I watch the two of them react to each other and I know that they were once lovers or maybe they still are. The blonde thin gentle leans over into Shaun as he talks to him.  You could see it was not an agreeable exchange from Shaun's side. Maybe he is worried that I will walk up and catch him in what is his real world.  The man's blonde hair rests in his face, every few seconds he would move it away from his eyes.  I watch as Shaun examines the intruder.  He is reading him and talking to him with more body language then with words. When I arrive, the man stands, he is taller then I imagined.  He is closer to Shaun's height.  He is introduces as Cedric and we shake hands, not in the way you greet someone for the first time, more of the fashion that you shake hands with a potential foe. I have questions but of course I do not ask them. I could see in his face I was much of curiosity to him as he was to me.  Cedric looks at me and smiles half heartily. He is rather attractive but then you would expect nothing less from a past love of Shaun. I was interrupting and he is not happy with that.  He looks at Shaun, then at me, he is not smiling anymore, his look has changed to disappointment.  Cedric says his goodbye and absconds from the table and I retake my seat.

After a few minutes of silence, I want to question him but I don't feel I have the right.  Shaun turns to me.
        "That was a friend of mine."
        Close friends?
        "Yes.  He wants to talk."
        You can go talk to him, I won't mind, I say but I do.  Even this early in our development I don't want to share him.  I was never one for sharing, I found that to be so ordinary and I was anything but. Shaun is starting to reopen things I just recently wanted to die.  I couldn't allow myself to be hurt again, so soon. It is strange for me to be in the middle of something I have no idea about.  Shaun and I have avoided all conversations of past loves. Every spirit that guided my soul was telling me to slow my grove, to relax but with Shaun it was difficult.  Slow down the song says, so I can love you better, I often wondered better than what.
        "I like where I'm at." I smile as we stare at each other.
        What?
        "Are you enjoying yourself," he asks.  I want to scream hell yes.  I want to reach across the table and pull him to me and give him s taste of how I really feel, instead I just say,
        Yes.

"Then act like it.  When I look at you your mind seems to be someplace at."

No, I'm definitely here.  For the next few minutes we don't say much.  Then a woman walks out from the shadows onto the stage and crowd begins to clap.  She introduces herself as Ilene.  She begins to ding, as the band remains silent.  Her voice echoes across the room, overpowering any conversation as everyone and everything seems to stop to take part in her voice.  Sultry, sumptuous, her voice is full of grace.  She brings alive the room as the band begins to give her background noise.  She has won the crowd over with every following note, taking hold of everyone. She was a soulful angel blowing life into the masses with every note that flows from her lips.  The angel finishes her trio of songs and the crowd cheers and rise giving her gift of praise.  When she is done she walks off the stage into the crowd, stopping every so often by nighttime groupies. She is courteous and grants from a distance artificial humility for their benefit.  She is a striking woman, tall, long legs that follow outwards from her slit in her blue dress.  Her breasts sit tightly in her dress showing them on top for view. She makes her way across the room, shaking hands, garnering kisses on the cheek until she makes it to our table, Shaun stands, and I follow his lead.

"Ilene this is my friend Gabe," with that she sticks out her hand and we make contact.

"It's nice to meet you," she says.

You have a beautiful voice.

"Thank you, damn I need a drink," with that Shaun waves for the waitress, she takes our drink order and quickly retreats.

"You finally brought your sorry ass down here," she says smiling at Shaun.

"I told you I would I would be here. You were terrific, almost took me back to when you would sing to me when I was a little boy."

"Did you really like," she asks almost begging for his approval.

"Of course I did."  With a look of satisfaction on her face, she brings her attention back to me, digesting my presence, then finally smiling.

"So did you bring him for me or you," she asks with a smile.

"Lele, be nice," Shaun says as she laughs and leans onto his shoulder.

"Alright, this time," she says. "There's a record guy here, he says he's

"There should been ten guys here, Shaun says". You could see the bond between them, a bond that appears special, and one that only grows out of the purest of love.

"Well I have to prepare for my second set. Shaun calls me."

"I will."

"If it doesn't work out with my brother, you call me too."

You can count on that.

"Hey you two, now go do your set," Shaun says laughing.

"He's cute Shaun," Ilene says as I blush. She makes her way back into shadows. Her walk is so elegant, she flows across the room, her dress caressing her body tightly but still leaving room for her body to glide. She is a beautiful woman and her beauty only eclipsed by her captivating voice. Shaun watches her and could not take his eyes from his sister. He turns to me when she disappears, smiles and says so much with his eyes my ears was booming from his silent conversation. We sit and talk, this time about his sister, but our body was talking about the rest of the night.

As we drive back toward the downtown area, I feel myself rising up, wanting to invite him home, or invite I back to his apartment. Instead I pull in front of his building; we sit in the car and listen to the music coming out of the radio.

"I don't want to go up."

It's late.

"Can I see you when I get back?"

Sure, I would like that. He reaches across the car grasps my hand as I stare ahead. I change my focus to him after looking down at his hand engulfing my own gently rubbing it with his fingers.

"It's been a long time since interesting was a part of my life."

Then it must have found both of us at the same time.

"Well Good you are interested, I was beginning to wonder, if I lost you somewhere along the way tonight." He had no idea how I want him, no he was unaware of my inward drool.

I like you just fine. With that he opens the door and exits. He looks back, the wind blowing heavily onto his body. He clutches himself, trying not to show just how chilly it had become.

"Good night."

Night.  He closes the door and I watch him enter the building.  I take a long deep sigh and drive off, hitting Lake Shore drive heading south toward my home.

I can't sleep; my thoughts are in every place but sleep.  It's so easy to be entranced by what someone says when they are fine as hell.  I have been lucky in life, finding Aries, even the situation with Simon had been good overall.  Most people who are lonely are lonely because they try to guard their hearts so much that they end of deflecting their happiness away. Unhappy people try to drag you down because they are unhappy is common place. Trust is something that is difficult to establish but it one of the most beautiful things two people can share.

The wind picks up outside my window.  The tree limbs blow heavily against my window, crashing with every other breeze. I lay in bed, still not able to sleep but not able to stay awake. I am somewhere between peace and disturbance.  My room is shadowed from the little outside light. It gives a presence that I hadn't notice before in this room. It felt as if someone is watching over me, someone was here with me.  I am being comforted, I am being healed. With each new day I am gaining a part of myself that I had lost.  My eyes begin to close as I was settling in to catch a few winks before the sun woke from its slumber. My eyes had fallen shut, when I was drawn back by a loud heavy sound.  I open my eyes and realize it is my phone.  I reach over and pick up the receiver.

Hello.

"Are you having trouble sleeping?"

Shaun?

"What, you have other men calling at this time of the night?"

That depends.

"We have to change that."  I smile at this. I am a walking hard on around him, even his voice work up my manhood.

So what's up?

"I just wanted to say goodnight again and hear your voice."

I'm glad you called.

"Good, you are going to watch the game this weekend."

Of course.

"Goodnight Gabriel."

Night Shaun.  I place the receiver back on the base and close my eyes, settling in for the night.

I wake up on Saturday morning and fix a pot of coffee and turn on my television to watch the X-men. It is my favorite cartoon, not that I watch many of them but somehow these action heroes were than just cartoons. I think I understand them, I relate to them on many levels, the obvious ones and the not so obvious ones.  Growing up I had loved the super friends.  They were all American, all my friends wanted to be Superman, Batman or Robin when they were added to the show.  I wanted to be Green Lantern, he had style, nice jewelry and he know how sometimes justice needed to be had any cost. This morning, I curl up on my couch and watch television, wrapped in my favorite green quilt. My doorbell rings, lucky it's a commercial break and I move to the door to answer it.  I open the door, Simone stands there cloaked in his winter gear.  I let him in and he walks into the kitchen fixes a cup of coffee. I sit on the couch in my Duke t-shirt and a pair of matching boxers and watch him.  He comes in sits down, looks up at me and smiles.

"I wanted to see you."

What for, it's been almost four months.

"Come on, don't act like that.  You know how I feel about you."

No, I don't, twice I allowed myself to fall in love with you and twice you made a choice to leave.

"That's not fair."

Maybe not but it's true. I'm tired of being so damn understanding.

"I've missed you." I try desperately not to let it show but part of me misses him too.  For all of the pain, he was a part of me.  I think when you get close to people they leave a impression on your soul, sometimes these impressions can be hurtful and damaging and sometimes they leave memories that are as lasting as writing a good article. Simon had left both. He leans over and gives me a hug and I hug back, we kiss.

This doesn't change anything.

"I know I just need to hold you, to be near you, I need you."

I can't go back there.

"I'm not asking you to, I just want one last time to remember what we had and what I let go," he says as he lips covers mine and our bodies begin to intertwine if our souls did not.

Laying on the couch in Simon's arms as he gently runs his hand from my head down my back, we don't say a word.  We both know this can not go any further.  My phone rings and Simon reaches up and hands it to me.

Hello.

"Do you miss me?"

Shaun, hey, of course I do.

"I just checked into my hotel and I wanted to call you."

I'm glad you did.

"We have a meeting in a few minutes so I can't talk long.

I'm glad you called.

"I'll call you tonight, will you be home?"

I'm not going anywhere.

"I'll talk to you then."  I hand the phone back to Simon, he hangs up.  We lay there for a few minutes, not knowing what to say to him, not knowing what he is thinking. I run my hand over his chest and lay my head against him, his heart was beating rhythmically.

"Who is Shaun?"

A friend.

"Is it serious."

I don't know, we just met.

"You like him?"

Yes, I'm sorry Simon.

"It's fine, I knew you would move on, I want you to, you can't help if I can't move on."

Don't do this.

"I'm not trying to cause trouble, I just, I, I don't know, I can't stop loving you, no matter how hard I try. I've never felt like this about anyone except you."

This can't happen again.

"I know."

You are so important to me but I can't be a part of choice between your son.

"You will never understand how important you are to me, I feel like I've been floating since… If things were different…"

…But they aren't. Let's just enjoy this moment.

"Our goodbye, once again."

It's never goodbye, you'll always be in my heart. I rise to meet his lips, parting his mouth with my tongue.  We hold each other tightly, not looking at each other, not wanting to let go but knowing that we had already done the letting go part, closure because that shared part of our lives is over. Simon would soon return to the life he had chosen.  People make choices that they believe to be for the best and maybe they are initially, but once you make these choices, you lose what they left behind; it will never be the same.  You can never recapture the joy because every time you look back seeing what you left behind can only bring you sorrow.

I wake up Sunday morning after a restless night and watch the Bears get mauled by the Lions.  Shaun had a good game, one hundred and eighteen yards and two touchdowns.  The team falls apart in the fourth quarter again, with a three point lead they give up two quick touchdowns and lose.  I want to go get something to eat but feel a light cold coming on.  I lie on my couch and try to get some rest to avoid the cold but I quickly fall asleep.  I am burning up, a high fever is controlling all of my sense, so when Kim calls, I ask her to bring me over some cold medicine. About an hour later, she shows up with my medicine and fixes me some chicken soup.  I watch her moving from the kitchen with my bowl of soup, reminding me of the time when I was twelve and I had the flu.  My mother the preacher's wife bring me a bowl of soup.  She had so much love in her eyes, the flowered red and yellow dress, flowing as she gracefully moves toward me, her hair flowing upward that day.

Kim stays the entire day, she is so attentive to me, I'm sure she must have had other plans.  She sits on the couch and feeds me soup and wipes my head with a damp cloth. My mother had a way of making me feel special, the way she seemed to listen to me as if I was the only person in the world.  She would gently caress my face, making me feel all warm inside. My mother, those thoughts I could look back on with warm thoughts. I was her son and she seemed so proud of that very thing, now it was different. I don't want to think of her the way she is now.  I want to remember the woman who held me when she knew I needed it even I never said a word.  I want to remember the woman who laughed at all my little performances as a child. I still remember her sitting on my bed, singing to me. *Yes, Jesus loves you, yes Jesus loves you, for the bible tells me so, little ones to him belong, they are weak but he is strong*, she sang as I leaned against her breasts and she held me with arms wrapped around me, wiping my forehead.  She sang and sang and I dozed off to slumber, knowing how much she loved me.  What a difference time can make.  They say men are the biggest children when they are under the weather and my age, I still had the urge to have my mother take care of me because there is nothing more comforting to a child then a mother's love.

Kim sits a pillow behind me and helps me up. She hands me the soup and I begin to eat.  I thank her. She tells me about her and Michael have decided to get pregnant, I was happy for them, then her expression changes.

What's on your mind?

"You heard from Simon lately?"

He stopped by yesterday.

"Really?"

Yeah, it's fine.

"He's suffering Gabe."

What am I to do with that?

"Nothing I guess, it's just that you haven't talked about it."

What is there to talk about, he made the choice he had to make.

"Michael blames himself; he thought he was doing a good thing, sending him here."

Michael can't blame himself, Simon made the choice.

"You still in love with him?"

I'll always love him, but I need a man who knows who he is and what he wants.

"Simon doesn't love her."

I know, but I was lost for a long time after Aries and I felt myself slipping back into that darkness, I can't lose myself again, not this time, not now. I feel myself tearing up but I fight them back and I tell Kim I'm tired and I lay on the couch.  She sits in the chair and watches television and I doze off.

When I wake up, I look across the room and the television is still on.  I move my eyes across the living room and asleep in the chair is Shaun.  I sit up and watch him sleep.  I smile and he opens his and looks at me, grinning back.

When did you get here?

"An hour ago, I called from the airport; Kim said you weren't feeling well so I came right over."

Where's Kim?

"She left, I told her I would take care of you, you don't mind."

Not at all. What did you tell her?

"Not much, but she was pretty surprise about me.

I didn't know if there was anything to tell.

"I don't want to be a secret, not from your family, I'm just not trying to be a poster child.

I wouldn't ask that of you.

"Come on, let me help you to bed."

Oh is the big strong football player going to carry me.

"Hell no, but you can lean on me, I promise I won't let go." Shaun helps me off the couch, I hold on to his broad shoulders and muscular arms as we go up the stairs. Shaun lifts me carries me up the last few stairs, I think I am going into shock. As we enter the bedroom, he sits me in the chair and pulls back the sheets, he sits my pillows together and I get into bed. He stands over me as I lay in bed; he sits down on the bed and faces me.

You're not leaving are you?

"If you want, I'll be here; I'll sleep in your other room."

No, I want you here with me. I close my eyes and I feel him watch me for a minute. What is he thinking, I have no idea but I hope it is good. Here is a man that I barely know but something is happening between us. We are attracted to each other, that is not in doubt but it is not just a physical motivation that is drawing us together, it was more. The connection was a higher level, we aren't rushing into bed, our friendship was developing, and you can't always find someone who will be there to trust and to love in the very end. He lies down next to me and I feel his energy. I am able to rest.

As I awake, I open my eyes and I do not see Shaun. I must admit, I was a little concerned. He was there when I went to sleep. I had awakened several times during the night and seen his face resting peacefully. I am feeling better; the combination of flue medicine, soup and Shaun has been the right thing for my cold and my soul. I get out of bed and walk down the stairs and look down at my living room and kitchen. It is so quiet. The light from the morning sun is beaming in, I spot Shaun's jacket still hanging up, so I know he is near.  I stand for a few seconds and the bathroom door opens and there he stands as I admire him, shirt off, arch in his back and a V-shape with sweat moisture on it.  He left the heat up all night; he had suffered with me through the night.

"I see you're feeling better."
Much, I'll fix breakfast. I go down into the kitchen and begin to prepare breakfast; I turn on V-103.  The morning sounds from the outside mix with the kitchen sounds.  The car horns amplifying the sound of sizzling butter as the pancake mix hits the skillet.  I sat the table and then remove two glasses from the cabinet and the orange juice from the refrigerator and pour two glasses.  I feel him watching me.  I turn to meet his eyes.
Thanks for staying.
"There's no place I'd rather be."
Have a seat, breakfast is almost ready.
"You don't eat breakfast."
I'll make an exception, I'm starved.
"You going into the office?"
No, I thought I would take it off.
"Then I'll spend it with you, if that's all right."
There's no one I would rather spend it with. Shaun is so relaxed and that tends to draw people to people like him.  When you find someone who makes you comfortable and not so uptight, especially if you are naturally that way, it makes them more attractive, more desirable.  He smiles at me as I place the pancakes into his plate and his eyes crinkle in the corners. He makes me tremble with every look.

We spend the rest of day talking, getting to know each other. There is no pressure, the conversation just flows.  We are so relaxed with each other. I find myself with him laying on me in between my legs, leaning against my chest, as I run my hand over the top of his smooth head.  Every now and then he looks up at me, quite smiling but more of wondering.  After a while he reaches up and grabs my hand and pulls it down onto his chest and cups it, holding on to it.  I feel his breathe against my arm, he has fallen asleep.  I find myself exploring this man on top of me.  He still has my right hand, so it is a solo exploration with my left.  I run my fingers casually over his ear lobes, down his neck, touching his lips ever so gently, reaching his bare chest, glossing over his nipples, rubbing his stomach, stopping momentarily at his navel.  My hand begins to move farther down as it was beginning to be difficult to reach but I press on.  My fingertips have reached the inside of his pants, when his hand reaches out and grabs mine.  He turns to me, with an enormous grin on his face, sexy yet amusement is what his lips give off.

"What are you doing?"

What does it look like?

"I see."

It's about time, don't you think?

"I'm in no hurry."

It's been almost five months.

"Maybe we should talk about it first."

I think we've done enough talking.

"I don't want to fuck, I want to make love with you." He says as my hand makes it's way inside his pants.

Can't we do both.

"Will it hurt just to wait?"

When have you ever waited for anything?

"I waited my entire life to find you," he says as he lays back into my arms and I wrap my arms around him, his tight body.  I feel his lips moisten my arm, sure I waited for Aries but somehow this felt a little different.  With other guys, I either wanted the sex or I didn't. Shaun wants to wait and I want Shaun so I guess I am willing to wait, at least tonight.

At the office the following morning, I sit at my desk, when Will walks through the door.  I haven't seen him since I received his message.  He walks through the door and I look up at him and smile.  I have no hard feelings for him but he seems uncomfortable. I turn back to my desk and notice Wilson watching me. He turns and rushes out the door.  Wills comes to my desk and hands me my mail and stands for a few seconds, I finally look up at him.

What is it?

"I just want to, never mind."

Will its ok, there's no hard feelings, it'll stay between us.

"I know I can trust you, it's not that."

Then what?

"I feel like I should explain."

There's nothing to explain.

"I decided to marry her."

If you're happy then I'm happy for you.  Truth is told I hardly though about him once we stop fucking, I wish him no harm.  I did know he was setting himself up for a failed marriage, if nothing else one filled with pain.  He has a hunger that he is willing to push down but sooner or later it would bubble back to the top. He would not be able to rid himself of that desire.  I knew I was not the first man Will had been with and I knew I would not be the last.  As he walks away, I feel a sense of release but also sadness for him.  He was caught in a world where what he desired was still not acceptable. He was young and still not ready for that reality, sometimes I must admit I feel that way.  No one wants to be looked at as less than a man but few of us have the courage to stand up and deal with the desire that we have, but truth is we will always live with someone else's label if we don't create our own.

At lunch I sit with Wilson who seems to be in a playful mood.  He laughs and talks about his wife and family.  While Wilson talks my mind wonders around the room, watching the people who inhabit this Italian bistro. The walls are covered with pictures of Rolling Meadows and exquisitely drawn sketches of various wind vineyards.  The wooden tables still remained with a scent of freshness that blends with the smell of pasta and finely aged wine. The waiters seem too bored with their jobs just adds a tint of realism to the place.  Everyone had dark hair and eyes with the exception of the one black girl and two black guys they all appear to look alike but if I look closer they had similar facial features also.  Wilson squeezes my hand, noticing my lost thoughts and recaptures my attention.

"What's going on with you and Will?"

What are you talking about?

"Are you two…"

…Don't be silly.

"Hey, I just asked.  Who are you seeing?  I mean we both know you aren't ever single for long."

That's just not true, not everyone feels the need to be with someone every minute of the day.

"Don't jump down my throat unless you are invited."

You don't want to go there; you are the one with a wife and kids.  He smiles and so do I.

"Yes, I know, so who is he?"

No one really.

"What the hell does that mean?"

It means none of your damn business.

"When do I get to meet him?"

Let me think about that. I finish my Alfredo and take the last sip of my wine; I think about Shaun, I wonder what he is doing right now. Here I sit with a married man that at one time I had shared my bed with and Shaun is probably getting his body rubbed down by some trainer.

Back in the office, I begin to work, kicking around my follow up to the Jesse Jr. story. It was a probe comparing FBI investigations into urban politics but not into smaller areas in the country, where it seems to be more corruption. My phone rings, I pick up, hoping it is Shaun, It isn't.

"You're an asshole."

Michael, what the hell is wrong with you?

"Shaun Sharpe and I don't even get an invite over."

Calm down dude, its football player not God.

"Yeah, what ever, my wife sees his picture and oh that's Gabe's friend.

I'm sorry dude.

"I can't believe you didn't tell me."

There's nothing to tell.

"At first I thought about killing you, you know for not letting me meet the second greatest wide receiver to play behind Jerry Rice."

All right I get it, why don't you stop by tonight, we'll hang out and bring Kim.

"I'll be there at seven."

Then pick up Chinese, I'll get beer.

"Cool, I'll see you tonight."

I hang up the phone and have to laugh. Michael seems more excited that I am seeing Shaun then I was. He was like a little child about to meet one of his idols for the first time. I smile at that thought.

"Tell me the joke", I gaze up to a warm grin from Reginald, "It must be really funny, you're pretty amused by it."

Reggie, what's up man?

"So you're going to tell me?"

It was my brother.

"I see."
I read your piece man, it was good.
"Just good?"
It was better than that.
"So what are you doing for Christmas?"
Nothing major, hanging with my brother and his wife.
"You're still coming to my party?"
Wouldn't miss it.
"Then I'll see you there," Reggie says as he stands up
and goes back to his desk.  He picks up his duffle bag and heads
to the elevator.  I watch him from behind my papers, as he
stands at the elevator. He turns back and peers in my direction,
he steps onto the elevator and smiles as the door closes with a
thud.

I was alone in the office; I wouldn't be coming back here until
after the New Year.  Not exactly my favorite part of the year but
somehow I feel this would be the start something new,
something different.  I decide I have had enough and begin to
gather my belongings including my notes for my next article and
place them in my brief case.  I pick up my bag and grab my
jacket from the coat rack and head to my car.

The wind blows hard, unsympathetically at the people who pass
in the streets.  I look in the faces of the people who pass and
stare with contempt of the cold weather.  Women clutching their
purse men hold their jackets closely and I cannot feel the least
bit of compassion. When I arrive at my car Shaun stands next to
it, he has a smile on his face and some flowers in his hand; he
leans over and kisses me on the cheek.
You're stalking me now?
"Damn straight, I paid the lady at the desk to give me a
call when you leave", he says laughing with fervor.  I unlock the
door and he slides into the passenger seat, as I walk to the
drivers' side to get in.  He reaches over and opens the door for.
When I was a teenager Michael told me about how he did that on
his dates.  He says that little test to see if they opened it for him
told him more about someone then spending hours with them.

We don't do much talking on the ride, Shaun just holds my hand.
When we arrive at my house it is a relief, I don't know how much

longer we can go with the rode we are on.  I park the car and turn off the engine.

We're here, I say as I reach for my door handle.

"Wait", Shaun says, grabbing hold of my hand, "After the game on Christmas, I'm going back to Washington to spend a few days with my parents, I told them I might have a friend with me, what I'm trying to asks is do you want to come with me."

What?  I stare at him and my eyes begin to swell up.  I couldn't speak, it seems that my vocal box has decided to take this precise moment to take a vacation.  This was a big move; I had only met Aries parents before this.  It's an important step in a relationship when you meet the parents.  It can either strengthen the bond or it can rip it apart.

"Is it something wrong?"

No, I'm sorry, I just…

"…If it's too soon, just say no." I lean over and place my hand on his cheek and I kiss him, using my tongue as the guiding post for the rest of my mouth.

I would love to meet your family.

"Woo, good, I was nervous, we'll be back New Year's eve."

So we could go to one of my friends' party.

"Sure I will go."

Do your parents know?

That you're black, I tried to break it to them, of course they know, my parents love me, all of me, besides I would never put you in a situation to have to lie to them.  The impression on his face let me see that I had found a man with honesty and integrity and my wall had loss another brick.

"Can we go inside I'm freezing."

Let's go.  We exit the car and make our way into the house.  He takes hand as we head up the walkway.  It feels really nice to feel intimacy again on a level that had been gone for nearly two years now.


An hour passes before Michael and Kim shows up.  They walk through the front door and Michael was more like a little boy then a grown man.  He shoves the food in my hand and scans the room for Shaun.

"Where is he?"

What no hello little brother, just where is he? Kim laughs.

"He's been acting like a nine year old on Christmas morning all day," she says.  Shaun comes down the stairs and Michael stands there, just staring.  Shaun makes his way to him and shakes his hand.  Kim and I walk into the kitchen with the food and we grab four cold beers from the fridge and come back to join them in the living room. I feel this is like when my mother and father use to have company and the women were stuck serving the men. I sure in the hell wasn't about to replace my mom. Kim sits down next to Michael who was leaning forward asking Shaun about the upcoming game and rehashing Shaun's earlier career. I make my way to the couch next to Shaun and listen to my big brother go on and on.  I haven't seen him so excited in a long time.  Finally Michael takes a breath and looks over at me and then down to Shaun's hand on my knee, by his expression he was curious.

"How did you two meet," Michael asks, looking past me to Shaun.  It was a clear sign that I should not answer.  Shaun looks at me then smiles and turns to Michael.

"At a benefit, about two months ago, he rescued me from this boring group of guys." I don't know exactly what Michael thinks of his reply.  I love Michael and as much as I know he loves me, I also know he doesn't quite understand who I am.  He accepts me and he loves me, I know that but every now and again, I see in his eyes he wishes I was somehow different.

After Michael finishes his drilling of Shaun, Shaun tells him he was glad that he got a chance to meet him and Kim and then informs them that I was going to meet his family on Christmas day.  I hear my stomach growl; I stand and go into the kitchen.  Michael follows me into the kitchen.  He offers to help fix the plates and warm the food, the silence is deafening.

What's wrong, I ask him as the laughter from the living room makes us both turn and look in that direction.

"Do you know what you're getting yourself into with this guy?"

What are you talking about?

"You've always been open about who you are, no matter what the cost, I don't think he can do the same."

I know who he is Michael.

"What you going to sit in the wives section?"

Don't be a smart ass, we're friends Michael, don't plan the wedding.

"I see the way he looks at you and the way he looks at him, I've only seen you look that way twice before."

You worry too much.

"I have to worry, as strong as you, I don't want to see that hurt in your eyes again."

Aries died, and Simon left. That is a part of my life, but I wouldn't change that part of my life.

"How much can one man take before he loses it?  Can you handle heartbreak?"

I can't stop living; I was dead for almost a year. I can't worry about future pain.

"I just love you so much," he says as he comes over and embraces me.  I didn't want to let go.  I want to hold on to him forever.  Michael has been the one constant in my life.  I am glad he is here, I am glad to have someone watch over me.

We sit around the table laughing and talking. It is a great evening.  Michael took hold of Shaun's attention, of course.  It is amazing watching him get so excited talking about sports with who he considered an expert. He actually gives Shaun advice, telling him how he thinks his game could improve if he runs sharper out patterns.  Shaun agrees but I don't know if it is out of keeping the piece or he really thinks the advice is valuable, I'll go with keeping the peace. I add my two cents occasionally but mostly I stare at Shaun, smile and watch his lips glisten with every word.  Sporadically, we lock eyes and he smiles at me.  Michael catches the contact and then briefly he smiles with his eyes, I think he is becoming comfortable with this promising love affair, my big brother, always the protector.

The rest of evening goes rather well, there was no forced conversation; it was if we had all been a part of each other's lives for years.  Michael and Kim leave around eleven thirty and Shaun helps me clean up the place.  I hate holiday music so we turn on the CD player and listen to one of my Nas albums.  We finish and it is midnight, I plop down on the couch to relax, Shaun comes over and slides next to me and lifts my legs and places them in his lap.

"You're really cute for a short guy."

It's late.

"That it is," he says as his hands rub my legs through my slacks.  His six four frame feels right holding my five teen frames.

I guess I should get my keys and take you home.

"You don't have to.

It's too late to call a cab.

"It's not too late for us to share the bed."

I thought you wanted to wait.

"I did, I mean I do."

I don't.  I want us to fuck.

"As long as we're making love at the same time."

Most definitely.

"Let's go to bed."  He stands up and pulls me up to him. My body is so close to him, he stares down and takes hold of my chin, placing his lips onto mine.  My body aches.   It is as if all my sense was reborn and I was feeling them for the first time.  I hold onto his hand tightly, guiding him up the stairs to my bedroom and into my bed.  I turn off the lights switch off on the left side of the living room with my left hand.

As we enter my room, I turn the light by my bed and begin to undress; Shaun walks over to me and helps me, stripping me down to my boxers.  I turn my back to him and he moves down and lowers them off my body and steps back.  I turn to him and he watches me.

What?

"You are so fucking amazing."

Shut up.

"I am so crazy about you. I must have done something right."  I climb up into bed and he walks around to the other side, passing the window, the light reflected off his body, exciting my mind but also leaving a picture.  I watch his brooding face and his wiry body lean over me and kiss me.  He slides in bed next to me slipping his arm underneath me bringing me to him, knowing we will not have to say a word; I feel his breath on my neck and flick my tongue out to him. I feel his excitement and I know this will be the first time we are joined not only in mind but now in body and soul.

## WHEN YOU LOVE SOMEBODY!

Shaun is still asleep, as I move downstairs to my work area to begin working on an article I was writing about family history and acceptance.  Eric had asked me to do something on family for the February issue which is quite ironic since my family is so chaotic. I didn't want to make up anything about my family so the piece was more about the importance of family. I used an experience when I was nine when I was being bullied and Michael made me stand up to him.  He threatened to kick my ass if I didn't and I was more afraid of my big brother, I wanted the article to be humorous.  I had just finished up and was proceeding to rewrites when my doorbell rings. I rushed to open the door, not wanting to wake my sleeping prince. Upon opening the door, I freeze as I glare into the eyes of the woman who had given me life.  She stands there with her bag tightly on her shoulder, staring back at me without saying a word.  Finally the silence is broken.

"Can I come in?"

Sure.  I let her through the door.  It is a weird feeling when your own mother feels like a stranger.  I take her coat and she stands near the front door, looking uneasy.

Have a seat.

"Thank you", she says taking a seat on my couch, I sit on the loveseat, not knowing what to say, so I wiggle my fingers.

What brings you here?

"I wanted to see you."

Oh.

"How have you been," she asks while all I could think was like she really cares.

Fine.  Is something wrong?

"I miss my son." she says. My mother and I had been close a long time ago. Things are different now, I always thought she would come around but so far that had not occurred. "I really want this to end," she says.

What do you want me to do about that?

"I don't know, maybe this was a mistake," she says as she stands.

I've missed you too, but it was you and dad who made the choice not to have me apart of your life, not me.

"What you have become almost killed us." I felt my flesh rising up; she comes to my home and begins to immediately blame me for this situation, not taking any responsibility.

I can't be anyone that I am not.

"You are not this, you are my son."

Let's not do this.

"It's hard for me and your father around this time not to have you as part of our family.  Your father will never admit it, he misses you so much."

It's hard to believe that.

"I want you to talk to this man, he's not a doctor but he's had success helping other men with your problem come to terms and get back on their right directions."

I don't have a problem.

"I know you don't think you do but you have to understand that this lifestyle is a problem."

If this is why you came, you made a mistake. I'm not asking you to become flag waving parents, but I am who I am and if you love me, but you can't do that.

"All we ever wanted was the best for you.  You're not happy, Michael told us about Aaron."

His name was Aries, and I was happy and I am happy.

"Just stop it."

I'm not the depressed faggot that needs to be saved.

"Don't speak to me like that."

Maybe this was a bad idea, maybe you should just go. I look at my mother and I want so badly just to take her in my arms and squeeze the pain away.  I also know that my mother no matter what she feels will always stick with my father.  I feel myself about to break down and I can't allow her to see this.

Maybe you should leave.

"Maybe I should," with this she stands.  I hand her coat to her and open the door.  She stands put it on and walks out of the door.  She doesn't even look back.


I close the door and I feel the tears begin to stream down my face.  A mixture of anger, disappointment and fear rake over me and I begin to weep.  It is all I can do not to just fall and lose total control.

"Are you all right?" I turn to Shaun standing on the stairs, in a pair of my gold and black gym shorts.  He looks at me with such understanding, acknowledging my pain.  He walks down and takes me into his arms and become my shoulder holding me up.  Raising my head, he wipes away my tears and kisses me. We don't see a word, I look up into his eyes and kiss him on the lips and he responds, sharply parting my lips with his tongue.  I move slightly away from him and we stare into each other's soul for what seems like an eternity and then kiss.  I lean my head into his chest, he comforts me. I begin to wonder what he is thinking.  We scarcely know each other and yet it seems that we have always known each other.  Here he was taking my sorrow as if it was his own.  In the months we have known each other we had begun to learn more about each other than most people learn in a lifetime. No guards, no confusion, baggage but despite it all there is a connection.  A deep bond that sometimes takes years but can occur in an instant. As we stand here still intertwined, I remember the words of the poet Max Ehrmann, "Remember", he said, "what peace there may be in silence."

It is Christmas Eve; I am packing my bags with the football game playing on the tube.  I must admit the nervous energy that I feel is giving my body a workout.  I just returned from exchanging gifts with Michael and Kim.  They are so happy, especially with the news that Kim is pregnant. Michael will make a great father and Kim is meant to be a mother and you can't say that about everyone. TOUCHDOWN, the announcer yells, as the Bears were having a good game I sit on the bed to watch the replay and then spot Shaun on the sideline smiling.  Men and their sports, I wasn't good enough for the pros but I spent high school and two years of college roaming the sidelines.  I was a walk on in college but I still had a chance to experience that uncompromising bond of team mates.

My doorbell sounds and I walk down and open it, a troubled face Simon stands at the front door  He looks at me, not smiling, like has so many times before. SO I take the leap and smile at him and ask him to come in.  There is a slight sigh of relief on his face, we haven't seen each other since we made love about the same time I met Shaun.  He notices the bags I had already brought down.
        "Where are you going?"
        Spending Christmas in Seattle. I had heard from Michael that things between him and Sara were not going well.  Although I feel sorry for him, I knew I can never go back. The solemn

mood makes me want to end this visit quickly.  I can't allow myself to get involved again in his life.  He looks at me and opens his arms just like old hat I enter them and he hugs me.  I back away.

Why are you here?

"I needed to talk to someone and I trust no one like I do you." He is in such pain.  I can see the desperation in his face.  I try to avoid his gaze but can't.  I still care about him, he was my first love.  We sit there watching the football game half-heartedly.

"So is it serious?"

Is what serious?

"You and Sharpe?"

Michael has a big mouth.

Don't be mad at him, I asked him.  Just can't we can't be together doesn't mean I still don't care if you're happy." I look at him wanting to shake him and tell him that he made the choice and he would not be happy with Sara because his heart wasn't there but I know that is not my place.

I don't know if it is serious.

"Meeting his family is a big step."

It would appear that way but we are both clear, it's a visit, nothing more. Why are you here?

"I wanted to see you."

We can't keep doing this; it's not fair to either one of us. We have to let go.

"It's easy for you, letting go."

No, it's not, but I have to.

"Sara can't take any more of this and neither can I.  All we do is fight."

I can't here this.

"I'm leaving her, for good."

I hope that makes you happy.

"I know you don't believe me or want to her this but I had to tell before you make this commitment to another man.  I love you Gabriel, it was never about Sara, my entire life has been about you, let me close this out with her so we can move forward together."

I can't go back Simon. No matter what excuse you have next, it'' never be about Sara or your son, it's about you and your fear of truly loving another man.  You broke twice and twice I had to glue myself back together, I don't think I can do it a third time.

"Not everyone can be as sure as you are as these things. Yes, I am afraid but I realize how much I love you."

I know.  If you are ready to be with another man, I wish you the best but I'm good and happy for you, I just understand I won't be that man. Maybe someone where down the line we can be friends but for now we should just say goodbye.

"That's how you really feel?"

That's how it is.  We stare at each other and he leans over and kisses me, takes his jacket and walks out of the door. Somehow I know this is not over, I can never really lock him out of my life but I had enough strength to place him on the other side of the door.

I go to the window and watch him walk down the porch steps to his door.  I realize how much I have counted on him to take the pain that was burning inside of me. In reality he had caused some of that pain and then turned into the band aid to stop the bleeding. The truth is Simon was the one I had been the medicine for. For all Simons' baggage he is important to me, he made me realize that even after Aries there was reason to keep going.  Simon was slowly dying and I hope that he now was ready to live.  Everyman has a choice of two paths and most of the time even when we choose the wrong path, eventually those paths will cross again and we'll have a second chance to get on the right one. The right path is the one often less traveled and filled with obstacles but this road, in the end, is the one with the greatest reward and the most happiness.

The plane ride into Seattle is full of turbulence.  Besides the guy next to me constantly talking, I put my headset on and fall asleep.  I had to keep them on most of flight to avoid his snoring. I don't know why but plane rides seem to be a breeding ground for obnoxious behavior that makes everyone else's ride as miserable as their lives but the flight wasn't that bad.  I encounter a flight attendant who offered to show me around if I took her to dinner. I tell her I would call if I get free. I like the attention, the subtle flirtation with women makes me feel good even if there is no follow through.

As I walk off the plane down the long dirty green carpeted terminal I feel a little discomfort.  I don't know if it is the long flight along with the urge to take a shower or if it is I am about to meet the parents. I will bet it's the latter. I emerge from the door into the airport and I look around and Shaun stands looking damn fine. A smile creeps across his face as I walk toward him.  He stands with another guy, a little younger than him but you can tell they are from the same gene pool.  I walk up to him and he grabs my bag, he turns to the young man next to him and introduces us.

"Gabriel, this is my little brother Shannon."

Nice to meet you.  Shannon reaches out his hand with politeness and a smile, a little shorter than Shaun and with hair, shakes my hand.  As we walk to baggage claim, Shannon hardly says a word and I am too tired to engage anyone in much conversation.  Shaun does much of the talking, giving me details about what he has planned for my visit.  This is my first visit to Seattle and I do want to explore the corners of the city.  Shaun is extremely proud of his little brother who plays football for University of Washington. As we walk a gentleman in a powder blue suit approaches Shaun with his young son asking for an autograph.  I watch Shaun give the autograph and engage the man and his son in brief conversation which puts a smile on the boys' face it feels surreal.

"So you write for Conurbation", Shannon asks as we stand back waiting for Shaun to finish.

Yes for over a year now.  I try to read him and what he is thinking, Shaun had told me Shannon took it the hardest when he told his family that he was gay.

"I have a subscription.  When Shaun said you and he were friends, I wanted to meet you; I really like your work."

Thanks. What did you think of the piece on the congressman?

"I thought you were too nice."

Well yeah, legal purposes and all some things had to be removed.

"It still was a good story.  So I guess you're nervous?"
How can you tell?

"Don't be, my parents are cool. You're the first guy he brought home for the holidays but when they met Cedric, they had no reaction other than the one they have for me or my sisters." I had met Cedric.

Then I guess I have nothing to worry about.

"I didn't say that."  Shaun returns and we continue our journey down to retrieve my bags.

The car ride is a little livelier; Shannon talks all the way home, asking questions about some of my past work.  We talk sports and they try to prepare me for what the holidays are like at their house. I watch the two of them interact and I miss my own brother and for a brief second wish I would have stayed in Chicago. The drive is pretty quick; at least it feels that way.  I admire some of the architecture of Seattle, from the grand houses that stand on top of hills to the Spanish influences on some of the smaller houses.  Seattle is a beautiful city, with the fresh rain that covers the streets, dripping from trees to the lake that lies around it creating a beautiful aura to the environment. As we pull into the driveway of a large villa style home, with an immense picture window, I feel a knot tie in my stomach. The car stops and we exit.  I begin to look around at the neatly trimmed yard and flower bed that covers both sides of the house. Shaun walks over to me and for a moment my fears disappear inside his eyes, that is until the door opens and a woman, who I assume to be his mother makes her way down the walk to the car.  She has a smile that tries to put me at ease but her eyes had questions and I was not sure I had the correct answers.  I reach my hand out to shake her hand but she pulls me close and hugs me instead.

"We can do better than a handshake, he's talked so much about you that I feel like we've been family for years," she says as she hugs away.  Shaun just smiles and stands there.  I don't know what to say, I  think I manage a grunt but my heart is pounding and I can feel an heart attack about to occur so I really don't hear much more.

"Well come on and let me introduce you to the rest of the family," she says placing her arm around me guiding me into the house.  This makes me feel more at ease but I was about the meet more of the Sharpe clan and this could just be a set for my slaughter.   The two brothers pull my bags from the trunk of the car as Mrs. Sharpe and I make our way through the front door.

Inside I look around at the décor; the living room is done in black with brightly colored paintings and multicolored pillows to liven up the room.  Over in the corner stands a baby grand with black and gold trimmings. The place is full of tall, short, big and small plants.  They are everywhere.  The floor was not carpeted but wooden, shining with a glow. With all the money that had been earned she still has the black mother thing, that her living room is her show piece and no one steps foot inside of it. I hear Shaun enter, talking to his brother but I cannot see him.  I am walked into a room where the television plays.  A man sits in the chair, watching an episode of the Honeymooners, Shannon enters the room.

"Dad turns off the TV. for a minute, this is Gabriel."  The man in the chair turns and I walk over to him and he rises from the chair and we shake hands.  He looks at me for a few minutes then takes his seat.  Shannon points for me to take a seat, so I oblige and sit on the sofa closest to his father.  Shannon and his mother exits and Mr. Sharpe and I sit there in silence.  A few minutes later it is broken.

"Don't let him scare you, he does this silent father thing all the time," a voice says as I recognize and turn to see the young lady, five foot seven, with short black hair and radiant brown eyes, looking at me smiling.

Regina.

"It is good to see my brother finally found some common sense."

Well I'm not quite sure of that.

"I hear you are back in Chicago."

Yes, where are you at? I haven't seen Regina in about eight year we started work around the same time at the Journal. She always talked about her family; I guess the world is small after all.

"It must be fate," she says with a wicked smile. The time we worked together we were extremely close.

Must be, I say to her with my heart reminding how all this had come at a high price.

"I was sorry to hear about Aries, it's two years now."

Yes.

"I remember how much in love you were."

"Who was in love," Shaun asks as he enters the room.

"Boy bring your big sexy ass over here."  Regina opens her arms and Shaun walks into them, rubbing her head and she gives him a light punch in the gut.

"Who did you love Gabriel", he asks again.

"Aries, I knew them back in Atlanta." I am glad Regina chimes in, letting me off the hook.

"The one you never talk about," Shaun says looking directly at me.

I guess we all have people we don't talk about. Shaun and I look at each other and Regina stands there.

"Well I guess I should be aware when I am about to start a war", Regina says attempting to lighten the mood.

"Where's dad?" We all turn to the chair which is empty.

"He must have went into his office," Regina replies.

"Probably grew tired of your ramblings."

"You know I can still kick your ass."

"Only if I let you," Shaun replies, "We'll talk later,' he says to her giving her a final squeeze, "You, come with me, I must show you were you are sleeping." He turns and I follow him.  We walk out the door and up the first stairs, down the hall to a spacious bedroom at the very end of the hall.  My suit cases are already resting on the bed and I walk over and take a seat as Shaun closes the door. He looks at me as he leans on the door.

What's wrong?

"Why don't you talk about Aries?"

What for?

"I love you, and I want to know everything about you."

Then what?  Shaun if I talk about him, then it'll seem that I am putting all these expectations on our relationship and I just want this to be about us.

"He is a part of us, because you loved him, past loves may walk out of our lives but they still remain."

You don't talk about Cedric.

"There isn't much to say."

I'm not the only one who's afraid of talking about the past.

"You're right, so what do you want to know."  He sits on the bed next to me and for the next three hours we talk about our past. We discuss our past and we finally tell each other about the hurt, the pain and the joy. We open up to each other and for the first time I expressed my deep love about Aries to someone without any pretense or holding back the tears.  He tells me about Cedric and how they started and ended and he told me for the first time in a long time he looked forward to the future and I could not agree more.  Shaun pulls me into his lap and we kiss. He lays me aggressively on the bed and begins to kiss me.

So where are you sleeping?

"Let me show you," he says as he stands and begins to undress.

I probably need to take a nap or something.

"Oh, I agree, but first let's work out a little sweat."  He leans back down on me and kisses me.  We work ourselves out of the clothes and into the sheets and our bodies feel right touching and sharing each other but this was more than the first time, it was intense and valuable.  It was the time that feels like a first when your heart knows it can speed up or slow down, but either way it knows this is something real.  It was the excitement that makes you feel at ease yet amplified.

I must have fallen asleep sometime after it, when I woke up Shaun is gone.  I hear a faint knock on the door then it opens and Regina stands with her head ducking in.

"You're awake."

Come in

"You and my brother?"

Yeah, can you imagine?

"What is funny I did, I thought you would be perfect for him, I just never thought it would actually happen."

Someone must have heard your thoughts.

"Well, my brother owes me for putting this out in the universe."

I think I might owe you too. How is Frank?

"We ended soon after I left, he was really insecure about too many things."

Is that good or bad?

"All things have their purpose."

"Do I have to worry about you two," Shaun asks from the doorway.

"Not at all, little brother, we're just catching up."

Well I don't know we do have a past. Regina hits my arm and we both laugh and Shaun smiles and walks crawls next to me on the bed.

"Did she wake you?"

"No, I didn't, I was just warning him."

"About what?"

You, what else?

"All right, I'm out of here," Regina exits the room, closing the door behind her.  Shaun inclines into me and kisses me with a soft gentle kiss.

"I told my mother that we would sleep for a while."

I'm wide awake.

"I was counting on that but I told her that so no one would disturb us, I have other things in mind.  I lift out of the comfort of the bed into Shaun, loving having his arms wrapped so tightly around me, with his lips embracing my neck. I want this week to be about me and Shaun.  We shared our history and now we can begin to make new chapters of the story that will one day be about our lives. I can feel and hear Shaun breathe and I knew that I was going to love him more and more each day and I only prayed that he would love me that way. His tongue flickers on my ear and I stop thinking about anything but this moment and for the second time in hours our bodies became one intermingled with each other and loving every sense that we were making together.

As we lay in bed together the clock read eight seventeen. As I try to stand Shaun pulls me back down onto the bed.
"Where are you going?"
Nowhere.  He lets me go and I go to the window to see the lady across the way pull up in her car and exit.  She reaches back inside her vehicle and removes a few bag and struggles to keep them in her arms with her purse as she tries to remove what I assume to be her keys. She makes it to her porch before all the bags crash to the floor.  I smile, I shouldn't be smiling but it is quite humorous.  Shaun comes behind me and embraces me; I wrap my arms around his and lean back into him.
"Maybe this is too soon, but I love you Gabriel, I think I did the first night I saw you, I think I always have." I know that I should have not do what I am about to do but I say it to him.
I love you too Shaun.  We stand in complete silence for what has to be ten minutes then we dress and exit the room, looking for sounds of intelligent life. Once again my heart was like an open wound, susceptible yet ready to be healed by someone's magic touch.

The rest of the night passes quickly and we eat dinner all of us. His father drills me over dinner, questions everything about me and then all seems fine, I guess I have answers that they find suitable.  I must admit this is what I have always wanted for my family.  I wanted my parents to know Aries and I know maybe it could have happened if fate had not stepped in and changed the course of my life.  Ten years with Aries and my parents never had the opportunity to meet him.  They never knew the one person who made me feel good and alive and who was the only person in my life to provide meaning to it.  Now I am on a different path and I realize that the meaning that Aries had provided for me was not for my mom and dad it was only meant for me and nothing they did or not did could change that.  We talked afterwards along with playing a game of charades.  Eventually Shaun's parents made their way to bed and we follow a few hours later.

I wake up in the middle of the night and Shaun is not next to me.  I look around the room and I still do not see him, so I proceed down the stairs.  I hear voices coming from the kitchen; I recognize Shaun and Regina so I pause.  I stand and listen knowing that I should not.

  "So you really like this guy," Regina asks.  There was a long pause.  What is he thinking, he'd better answer quickly.

  "Yes, I do and what's funny is that I know he likes but I love him and I don't know if he loves me."

  "Shaun comes on, Gabe loves you, I see it when he looks at you."

  "From the first night, I knew that he was the one."

  "What about Bradley, is he out of your system?"

  "God I hope so."

  "Have you talked about Brad with him?"

  "One ex at a time, Cedric was quite revealing enough besides Brad is here in Seattle and I am in Chicago with Gabriel."

  "If you had to choose, which would you pick?"

  "Brad and I don't work outside of the bedroom, with Gabriel I feel whole, I've never felt that before.  Did I love Brad probably always will, but I'm not in love with him?"

  "Gabe is a terrific guy, you're a lucky man."

  "Yes I know, tell me about Aries."

  "When I met Gabe, I would flirt my little ass off to get his attention and he was always polite and would return the flirtation, but then I met Aries, he was a beautiful man, but inside and out, Gabe has layers and layers of bricks that surround his heart but Aries quickly walked through them. If you and Gabe have half the passion that the two of them shared, you will be a lucky guy."

  "Aries sounds like a great guy."

  "He was but so are you.  Do you know how Aries died?"

  "No, he hasn't told me that."

"Shaun he was there, when Shaun was murdered, he died in front of him."

"What."

"In his arms, he watched while the man he had loved for ten years dies and he could do nothing about it. Most people never recover from that."

"How was Aries murdered?" I take a few steps back and call out for Shaun.  I have heard enough.  I shouldn't have ease dropped but I'm human after all.

"We're in here," Shaun calls out.  I walk into the kitchen and smile as Regina walks to Shaun and kiss him on the cheek, say goodnight and exits.  I walk to the sink and grab a cup out of the cabinet over it and go the refrigerator and pour myself a glass of water.  As I am sit the pitcher back in, Shaun comes behind me.

"Let's go back to bed."

All right. With that I finish my glass of water and we head back up to bed.

The next day old man Klaus made his yearly visit.  After spending time with Shaun's family watching them open gifts, watching my past as it was.  I become a little overly sentimental in this holiday cheer.  I excuse myself and walk into the kitchen; I sip on a cup of coffee, staring out of the window while I tap the side of the cup.  Shaun's father must have come in behind me, I don't know how long he had been there but he startles me with a cough and I dissipate some of the hot java on my shirt.

I didn't hear you come in.

"Sorry about that. I guess this is hard for you."

What do you mean?

"Shaun told me about your parents."

It's all right; it's been over ten years.

"No need to pretend with me son, family is important to me and Shaun, so I can only imagine what this time of the year is like for you."

No really, I have my brother.

"There' nothing like having your mother and father, come sit with me." As I sit down at the kitchen table, I feel a sense of strangeness over take me. I don't want this conversation, I want to escape but most of all I want cry. As much as I like to tell myself that my parents deciding I could no longer be in their life was no big deal, I still longed for parental approval.

Yes, I miss them but I can't change how they feel.

"I had a hard time accepting Shaun, it almost destroyed me and would have if I had let. It felt as if my son had died, then I realized that Shaun had not changed just my information about him.  Parents sometimes hold their dreams and hopes for their children and then they realize that your children aren't born to live for us, and they'll never be who we think they should be but we have to love them for whom they are. I'm sure in time your parents will come around."

If that never happens?

"Then you'll have a family as long as you want it.  My son cares for you and I trust Shaun so if he loves you then there must be a reason."

Thank you for that.

"Enough of that, I hear you met our wayward daughter Ilene."

Yes, she's a beautiful woman.

"She couldn't be here this year, tour or something."

Her new record label.

"Yes, overseas." I look up and Shaun stands in the doorway.  He just stares at us; his father turns to see what I am looking at. "Let me get back", Mr. Sharpe says standing and exiting.  Shaun enters and sits down he reaches for my hands and squeezes them, gazing into my eyes. I know at this point that I am a goner; I am in love with this man.

Later, Shaun and I exchange gifts.  I had seen this painting of two African warriors, lying beside each other in the middle of a battlefield. There were explosions in front of them, bodies lying bloody beside them and they were reaching out for one another, fingertips almost touching, their arms stretching as far as they could but the expression on their faces made it seem they were miles apart even in that short distance.  What caught my eyes were the look in their eyes, yes they were warriors knowing that death was upon them but the look in their eyes was not fear, it was more than comrades it was pure, it was love.  Shaun opens the present and looks up at me.

What?

"I love you Gabriel, I don't care that it's only been a few months, I don't care."

Shaun…

"...I know we have so much to get to know about each other."

...Shaun.

"...I just know that my life is more having you apart of it."

...Shaun!

"What?"

Shut up. I lean into him and I kiss him. It is an enchanting kiss, one that tells the two people involved that although we cannot be unsure of the future, it is this moment.

I unwrap my present, it is a copy of James Baldwin's novel, Go Tell It On A Mountain; it was in pretty good condition.

"Open it," Shaun says, so I do and the first page has an inscription, "To my love, may you read this in eternal peace, Jimmy Baldwin." I look up at Shaun with disbelief in my eyes.

"You mention how much he influences you, I think you said how you and he were soul mates that happen to born in different eras, so when I came across this I couldn't resist."

Thank you. I place the book on the night stand and rise into his body. I could not have felt any stronger for him at this stage. His body was pressed firmly on top of me and we were molding ourselves into each other.

The rest of the week Shaun shows me around the city. It was at the same time dirty and beautiful. I don't know if it was the city or the company but there is a sense of magic around it. We shop at Fishermen Market, look through antique book stores, purchase some classic Nina Simone and Sara Vaughn CD's. We drive around his old stomping grounds, and I listen as he tells me about each place and what moment in his life they represent. We even visit the place where he lost his virginity, behind this warehouse in his father's Buick. Shaun's family is great. They embrace me as only a black can do. There is none of the awkward formalities that can surround the invasion of people into families especially when it comes to acceptance of a same sex partner. The Sharpe family is warm and loving, while inclusion was the main stay of their policy. His mother continues to tell me about Shaun and all the trouble he would get into as a teenager. I am enjoying my time here with this family it almost makes me forget my own.

Tonight is our last night and Shaun takes me to the Space Needle. As we rise to the top, glancing out into Seattle's night sky, we gaze into each other's eyes, trying not to let go of every moment. Neither of us wants this to end and it wouldn't as long as we were together.  There is deepness with each look we share and the electricity that glows from an accidental brush of our arms made this moment only ours.  That is the thing about experiences, once you have them no one can take them away. They belong to you, unlike life itself; no one can take away your memories.

## Return Trip

On the plane ride home, it's New Year's Eve and we both sleep.
I am tired, it was emotionally draining and liberating for me to
visit with Shaun.  We arrive in Chicago and make our way back
to my place. We drop the bags and head straight to the bedroom
where we both collapse onto the bed.  I am awaken by Shaun as
he whispers in my ear,
      "It's time to have to sex." I smile on my face and I quickly
woke from my slumber, I open my eyes and say to him,
      We have to get dress for Reggie's party, so don't even
think about it.  He laughs as I stand and stretch, reaching for the
sky. Shaun reaches and pulls me to him.  This just feels right, I
know it and he knows it. I led him to the shower and as the water
begins to spray, he pulls my shirt over my head and I turn and
unbutton his pants and let them fall to the floor. We undress and
enter the shower and I feel his rigidness behind me and I know
he is ready. I want to make love to him at this very moment.  We
can b a little late for the party but something inside me was cold.
I should feel warm with him rubbing against me, his hands
lathering my body.  I decide to touch him and lean in and kiss his
lips, tasting him.  He kisses my forehead, my ears, down my
neck.  I want to stop him but I can't.  As his tongue runs over my
nipples and he begins to ingest them between his lips, I begin to
arch my body and he leaves my left nipple and goes to my right.
I am so incredibly driven to let him continue. His lips move over
my stomach, making sure to touch every inch of my chest, his
tongues darts inside my navel and I know if I don't stop here, I
will never stop him; I raise him up and open the shower door.

We stop out of the shower and dress; I watch Shaun dry off and
put on his clothes.  I think about him a lot, even though it had
been a short period, I feel I know him.  Then why am I so
cautious with him. I feel inadequate around him, watching him
get showered with so much attention the entire time we are in
Seattle, I was lost in his glory and although I know on a
conscious level that is not his doing, it makes me wonder, if this
will work. I am letting my insecurities take over or maybe it is that
he reminds me so much of Aries, from his sense of humor to the
gentleness of his kiss and touch.  The thought of being with him
seems a daunting task. We kiss a few more times, finish
dressing and make our way out of the front door without much

conversation.  Our drive is full of sexual nervousness and
moonlight stares. Our eyes meet and our bodies communicate
on a fathom wave, I try to pay attention to the road and keep his
hand from caressing my slacks but my dick gives me away and I
give in and let him touch me while I drive.  He stops when I run a
stop sign after momentarily because the pre-cum had begun to
leak inside my underwear.

"I guess I'll stop now."

That's a good idea.  We arrive in front of the house.  I
reach in the back seat and grab the wine I had removed from my
collection at home. It wasn't an expensive brand but I'm sure
they were already drunk as Ernest & Galio would suffice.

As we enter the house, I look around but I don't think any one
notices me their eyes are glued to the man towering above me
by my side.  Smiles and whispers begin as we make our way
across the room.  I spot Reggie standing across the room with
this woman laughing.  Heterosexual, I think.  His arm is draped
around her as he looks at me and smiles and she laughs at what
I suppose was a joke from the other man that stands in their
collective.  Wilson stood by himself as he smiles and I wave and
feel Shaun's hand brushing my waist. I peer around the room
and watch a strange unfamiliar man pour a glass full of bourbon
and sit it down in front of the rather attractive woman in front of
him.  She stares into the gleaming glass, thinking don't let it
happen, don't let me get drunk and go home with this man, I
think.  The lights clamor around his head as the whole bar lurch
forward to embrace her. Faces wave around Shaun as the music
from the radio pound into the room.  I turn to Shaun who was
looking down at me.  His soft eyes begin to move close to me, I
could smell his aroma.

A dark complexion woman walks up to us with his breast lifted up
for attention and her legs sliding across, she extends her hand to
Shaun.

"Shaun Sharpe, Vivian."

"Nice to meet you," Shaun says.

I'll be right back.

"Where are you going?"

"Let him go, I'll kept you company," she says grabbing
hold of his arm, putting him in her vice grip and she was not
going to let go easy.  I smile and make my way across the room

to Wilson.  He stands alone, like he had no real interest in being here. I touch his arm and squeeze it.

Where's the wife?

"She's at home. I see you got Shaun to join you."

Nothing good sex can't do.

"Looks someone else is trying to find that out."

Yeah, a little aggressive.  I stare at Shaun, watching the lady pull out all her tricks to gain his regard.  She tosses her hair, shoves her breast a little higher laughs at every word that comes out of his mouth and I know he's not that damn funny.  He looks at me and mumbles "save me". I excuse myself from Wilson and walk over to Shaun and put my arm around his waist.

Thanks my keeping him company.

"There was really no need to rush back," she says.

No, you're right but then again you can never leave your boyfriend alone that long at a party, now can you?

"Your what?"  She glares back and forth between us, "if you'll excuse me," she says making her way across the room like someone had stolen her fried chicken right out of her mouth.

"You know that was mean," Shaun says with a smirk.

Yeah, I know. I look across the room as Reggie and the woman approach us, still holding on to one another.  He approaches and we all shake hands as Reggie introduces us to Nadine.  What an incredibly awful name I think.  Sounds like some West German crack head stripper from one of those dusty joints near the airport.  She is nice and the four of us talk for a few minutes.

The party drags on and I spend most of the night watching as both men and women take turns mauling Shaun.  I talk to those I know and I even have a brief flirtation with some Latino guy.  Someone during the night I realize I have been watching Reggie and Nadine. I drink and walk and drink and walk.  It was a wonderful even, so wonderful that I couldn't possibly wait for it to end. As midnight approach I look for Shaun and find him yet again in some corner talking the faults of a four and twelve team. I look at him and smile and he pushes his way ever so gently from his fans and makes his way to me.

"It's almost midnight."

Yes, I know.  I have a feeling that this year will be different.

"Once it hits, can we get out of here."

You have to get home.

"Yes, we do, I have an idea how I want to spend the first hour of the New Year."

I think I might like that.  The countdown begins, ten, nine, eight, I realize that this moment is special and the more I try to stop my heart this man is just locking it up. Seven, six, five, can I really be in love for a third time in my life, I was lucky just to have one love. Four, three, two, most don't even find it once. One, I reach up and take hold of his face rubbing my fingertip over his lips, he leans down, kissing me until my toes curl and he takes half my spit into his mouth.  The first day of the New Year, I am with this brilliant beautiful man and my first thought was how much I missed Aries.

Let's go. With that we were in the car and make our way back to my place.

As we enter the apartment, I hold his hand locking the door behind us.

"You're quiet."

Am I?

"We don't have to do this."

I want to.

"You're thinking about him, you don't have to hide that from me."

Thank you.

"He was important to you, I just hope one day that I can be that and I can spend the rest of my life with you."

I'm falling in love with you.

"I've been falling in love with you since the first moment I saw you." I reach for his hand and guide him to my bed.  We undress quickly.  I kneel down and lower his boxers. I am face to face with the head that does most of the thinking for most men.  I rub it as he moans and my mouth covers it, engulfing it whole, then pulling back to the head, licking around it, taking it back down my throat. He puts his hands on top of my head and leaves them there, rubbing my cheek with one and caressing my crown with the other. I stand up and pull him in to me, our mouths meet and our tongues collide, gliding in and out our mouths. I can feel the base under his tongue, the attached muscles throb with such ferocity. He caresses me as I caress him, gliding my tongue over his neck across the face, across his lips, over his ear where I begin to suck on it as he moans.  My hand cups his ass, running my finger across his crack, I stick one inside, he whimpers, partially in pain, mostly in delight.  I pump his ass with my finger; he slides around, rocking back and forth on my hand.  He is so tight.  He moans and begins to dig his fingers into my shoulders.  He places his mouth over min, as my finger continues to invade his core.  Out legs wind together, our bodies sweat, our breathing coincides with one another.  I roll him over onto the bed and spread his legs as I lay on top of him, my hard dick caressing the outside of his ass grinding on him as he holds on to me.  I kiss and kiss, licking his back, sucking his neck, lowering myself, spreading his ass to taste his, the taste is so damn good. I spend so much time, sucking and diving in with my tongue.  His moans keep my pace constant.  I reach over and open a bottle of Wet and press my finger tips that are now lace and moist into his ass.  He pulls a condom out of the drawer next to the bed and opens it as I continue to massage his most welcoming place.  He pushes me over and places the latex over my hard dick and I ran my hand over it to lube it up. I slide on top of him facing him, I lean down and kiss him as I hold one of his legs above my shoulders and move upward into him.  I feel his fingers burrow into my shoulder. Inch by inch, slowly first my dick is being surrounded by his inside and I feel him melt onto me.  I stop for a second, look into him and lean down and kiss him.  I begin to rock back and forth, entering him more and more, increasing and varying my pace.  The pleasure on his face has change from the earlier grimace.  He begins to move onto me taking my fullness inside him.  He pushes backward lodging me into him I am filled with glorious anguish, he continues to rock taking me along for this journey. We fuck until we are spent.  The sheets are wet with our sweat, and cum.  We lay together on one side my ass to his dick, still throbbing from him entering me.  I hold his arm and feel his lips on my back as I place mine onto his arm. Every few seconds his lips would cover some other portion of my back.  No words said, no talking, just intimacy, just intimacy, just intimacy.

I must have fallen asleep because when I awake, the light was shining through the bedroom window.  I move around to face Shaun and he moves to greet me as I lean over to kiss him, he moves away.

       "Morning breath."

       I don't care.

"No, I mean yours."

Shut up, I say laughing and pushing him off the side of the bed.  He holds on and pulls me taking control and we land on the floor, he is now in control and we kiss.

Las night was something else.

"Give me a second and let's see if we can make it any better." We laugh.  We get back on the bed and he begins to massage my shoulders as I groan in delight, his hands are strong, so sweet and gentle.

"I have to go to Dallas this afternoon."

What?

"Yeah, I forgot to mention but the team left a message yesterday."

When will you be back?

"Two days, I'll call when I'm back to town and I'll come directly here."

You'd better.  He continues to massage my body as I continue to enjoy it.  It soon progresses to another round off love making.


We stand in the shower, just holding each other.  I walk to the front of the shower and let the water hit my face.  My mind seems to be standing on a cliff, staring into the wilderness, seeing a kingdom where Aries still exist.  I turn to face Shaun who stands with his back against the shower door.  His eyes are filled with despair; they are a reflection of my own.  Shaun takes my hand and pulls me into him.

"Baby I'm trying.  I can't make you forget but I want to make it better."

It's a rough day Shaun.  I lost him today, it's hard but it get's better, you make it better.

"You can love him and miss him and still love me, you never have to hide that.  Why are you pulling away?"

I'm not.  I was, and he pulls me to him roughly as he could.  I think he had expected me to resist, but I don't, I can't. He begins to touch my body. It was so beautiful, the way his hands roam over me.  I am feeling his tenderness at a higher level; everything seems to take a very long time. He begins to kiss my chest and suck on my nipples, tasting, nuzzling them as I moan.  He pulls away and steps out of the shower bringing me with him, our bodies dripping wet.  He gently lowers me to the floor, lying on top of me.  He holds me tightly at the hips, my hands exploring his muscled back. He rolls over and pulls me on top of him, massaging my as, cupping it rubbing his finger over my bud.  I feel the both of us both of us begin to rise.

The medicine cabinet.

"Aren't we prepared for all occasions?"

Just let me get the damn condom.  I jump up and open the cabinet and remove it, tearing it open, I slide it down on his hard member and I slide myself onto him.  I feel my body shake as he pushes his way upward into me.  IT hurts like hell and I think for a second I am going to scream.  My opening was not as lose as he had made it last night and my body tenses up which adds to the tightness.  He rises and kisses me, I catch my breath and I press down onto him and whimper in delight.  The room begins to fill with the steam from the shower; I bounce up and down as we take a joyous excursion.  I explode without touching myself it could be from the steady friction or it could be the way his dick fits inside me, arching itself to hit the spot.

After we shower and eat something, we cuddle, talk and just listen to music.  He has filled my life up so quickly that he scares me at times.  He is quickly becoming an important part of my life and no matter how my brain tells me to slow down, my heart this was not a fight to fight because I will only lose.  My heart is winning out.  Shaun makes his way to the front door holding my hand and his suitcase. He sits down his suitcase and pulls me into his arms, looks at me in they eyes and says these three magical words,

"See you soon', and with a kiss and a wink he is out of the door.

I go back to bed and sleep, dreaming about Shaun, Aries and my parents. Being with Shaun and his family has placed an importance in my life.  I want my entire family back.  I want to be with my parents and have them love me. I want to hear my father say I'm proud of you. In your dreams you can live an entire lifetime.  You can also live the perfect life, full of love, hope and affection.  It is a place where you control destiny, at least most of the time. The problem with dreams is you have to wake up.

When I wake up, I fix myself some noodles and sit down to eat them.  They are really awful, slimy and cold by the time I find myself eating them.  I sit in the living room watching the

championship game of college football, sipping on a beer.  The
doorbell rings during half time.  I'm not expecting anyone but it is
more of a surprise because here stands Simon, looking terrible.
He looks as if the weight of world is on his shoulders, his eyes
carrying their own set of luggage. He looks so pitiful or sad,
which is probably a better way to describe him.  I want so badly
to know what is bothering him but I am happy and as selfish as it
might sound I don't want him to ruin that.  I want to close the
door and send him away but I can't. I cannot be that cold, I could
see all the anguish that he is going through, I can't add to that.

He enters my apartment and sits on my couch.  I stand staring at
him for a while before I sit down.  He doesn't say a word.  I am
concerned but I don't want to be involved, truth is even when you
are no longer with someone you love, you just don't stop caring,
it just means you can't care in the same way. I finally ask him
what is wrong and he puts his face in his hands and begins to
weep.  I sit next to him and pull him to me as his tears begin to
flow into my Chicago jersey.
        "I left her, for good. It's over.  All I've done is hurt people I
care about, all I've done is hurt you."
        It's all right Simon, I survive, we survived, and it's good.
        "No, it's not, I've lost you, I ruined the one good thing in
my life besides my boy."
        Simon, you don't have to do this.  You said you left her;
take this as a chance for a new beginning.
        "That won't include you. Does it?"
        It can't, I'm sorry.
        "I understand.  I need a favor."
        What?
        "I need to stay here a few nights."  I stand up, how could
he ask me such a thing, I ask.
        That's not a good idea.
        "I don't have anywhere else to go."
        Go to a hotel, to Michaels.
        "I know this is a lot but I can't be alone right now and I
need you."  I look in his eyes and all those dreadful things that he
had done to me are wiped away by all those feelings that I still
have, to some extent for him.  I walk to him and he wraps his
arms around my waist as I wrap my around his head.
        All right, you can stay in the spare room.
        "Thank you.  I need a shower."

You know where everything is. Simon goes up the stairs. I sit on the couch. What am I doing? This was way beyond the scope of my duty as his ex. I have allowed him into my house. I have allowed him to place himself in the middle of my life once again. All I can think is he had to be gone by the time Shaun returns.

After a while I hear the shower running and I turn up the television and watch the end of the game. I really can't get into it. I keep thinking about the entire situation and tell myself what I am doing is a good and noble thing. After the game ends, Simon comes down the stairs wearing a pair of my Columbia shorts, his chest glistening from the shower, the towel wrapped around his neck. He is playing me like a flute and I a, following him like children to the Pied Piper. He sits next to me and smiles and begins to watch the television. I can smell him, his scent coursing out of his body. He sits arm on the top of the couch and moves it around me.

Simon it's not going to happen.

"We're friends; I just want to be close to you."

Don't do this; I'm not that little boy anymore.

"I know that."

Then don't treat me like it. I want to be your friend, leave it at that. If you ever care about me, then don't cross that line.

"I just want to hold you, nothing more."

There's always more with us, that's something that will never change.

"I know, neither will my feelings for you." I sit back on the couch. He moves to the other end. If I can get through one night without falling in bed with this man, I will get over this pull he has on me, I think to myself. Despite everything, I must admit that Simon has always held a special place in my heart. Until I met Aries, I never really believed anyone could co-op his position in my soul. I tried so desperately to explain those emotions nothing more than a little kids' fantasy about love. He was engraved in my soul for such a long time that nothing else seem able to replace them. Even we he devastated me and I reacted by sharing beds with many people as I could, I would still feel his touch only brought to the reality that it was another cold unimportant body in my bed at the end. Simon destroyed my innocence with his rejection and his refusal to admit that he loved me but now that he did fate still wouldn't allow us to be together because I couldn't chance the fact that even now he would feel the guilt of our love and return to her and once again make my heart break into a thousand little pieces. The doorbell rings.

I walk to the door and answer it.  Sara stands, cold faced, wrapped in a brown coat.

"Where is he", she asks, pushing pass me, seeing him, she stops and stares at him.

I'll be upstairs.

"Yes, please go somewhere," Sara barks out.  I look at Simon and he nods his head.  I walk up the stairs. Sitting in my room, I can hear the accusations flow from her mouth.  I can hear him tell her that they are done.

"This is my fault", he says, "I made a mistake and now I am trying to correct it."

"Is that why you are here", she says, "I know since you came back here on Thanksgiving, his birthday this would be where I would find, it always comes back to that faggot."

"I'm that faggot", he says "This isn't about Gabe, this is about us.  You deserve someone who can love you in ways I will never be able to."

"Do you love him?"

"Sara please don't do this."

"Do you love him", she says pausing after every word.

"Yes, I've loved him for fifteen years.  Is that what you want to hear", he says as she begins to cry, "Sara please".  I think to myself he's loved me that long, my God he had things could have been so different for us, but God had given us a second chance and he still didn't take it. I was shaken from my thoughts by Sara's voice.

"Stay away from, I hate you."

"I'm sorry; I just want to make it right."

"Why Simon, why did you do this to me, you loved him on our wedding day. You promised to love me until death knowing you didn't love me then."

"I did, I do love you, and you're the mother of my child.  I was so scared Sara and I know that doesn't make this easier."

"So now you get to walk away in the sunset with him?"

"No, I've hurt him too much."

"So you've just hurt two people that you claimed to love, you're just pitiful and pathetic."

"I'm trying to do what's best for everyone."

"I guess should applaud you," POW, I jump to my feet and rush out of the room. Standing on the top of the stairs I see Simon, lying on the ground, choking on his own blood.  Sara kneels beside him, holding the gun, crying, screaming in agony. Simon is surrounded by blood that seeps into the wooden, floor, I am frozen. She looks up at me, points the gun at me, tears streaming down her cheek, I cannot move. Simon is coughing and moaning, blood pours from his throat.  I am both scared and mortified. She stares at me, wipes a tear from her check, dragging blood across her face with each stroke, she stands up and begins to move to me, my hearts beats so loudly, I am sure the neighbors can hear it. She comes closer and closer.

"This was for the best; he can't hurt either of us now."  I wanted to rush to Simon, to help him, I took a step down the stairs and she raised the gun higher at me. I stop and she begins to pull back on the trigger, I close my eyes, knowing that this is going to be my last thought and I tell my brother that I love him and Kim, I tell Shaun how grateful I am to have loved him and I tell Aries I am coming to be with him then POW, I jump, hear a thud  but soon realize that I am not injured and I open my eyes, I see Sara on the floor, blood leaking feverishly from her head with remnants from her skull all across the floor next to her body. I walk upstairs to my room and dial 911. Darkness takes over me.

## LIFE MAKES NO SENSE, Damn it

When I wake up I am in a white room, I assume to be a hospital. A nurse is checking my pulse.  I look up at her.

"He's awake", she says as I look behind her to see Michael and Kim standing. I sit up and reach out to my brother, praying it was a bad dream, knowing it isn't. I hold on to him tight as I try to cry but my eyes do not give in to this wish. I still don't speak, I don't want to speak, if I speak then it is more real, it is more painful.

"It's going to be all right," Michael says, "There are some police officers outside and they want to talk to you." I nod my head no and turn away from them, lost in a world of sadness and sorrow, I cannot believe this is my life, I cannot believe I am living this nightmare.  They say God never gives you more than you can handle, then dear God why have you forsaken me. Sometime later I am being questioned by officers as I regain my sense of speech, at least long enough to answer their questions. They move away from as I hear Michael fill in the missing parts. I fall back sleep.

I am released and return to Michaels place.  I go directly to bed and do not move.  I laid here for hours before I can even think of sleep. I keep seeing Simons' body. Then I remember Aries bleeding to death in my arms.  It is a nightmare, not a dream, this is not supposed to be my life, and this was supposed to be a fresh start. Once again tragedy is thrust on me. Once again someone I love is no longer here and I had the privilege of seeing them taken away. Once again life had fooled me and pretended as if it would leave a smile on my face only to be cruel and take it away and guide me down another path of heartache. Once again my soul is crumbling.

I was standing with Aries; we were alone in the stairway of our apartment building.  We had just come from a party.  It was two thirty in the morning; I remember the time because I had just received a page from work.  I told Aries I had to go return the call but he wouldn't let me, he kept holding me against the wall. His hands held min above my head and he was kissing my neck. I was half-heartedly begging him to stop but showing no effort of pushing him away. It was officially our ten year anniversary. He begins to kiss me, we hear the door down the stairs open, Aries says it's just neighbors and since no one lived in the vacant apartment next to ours no one would come up this far, so he continues to kiss me.  He reaches inside my pants, I begin to giggle, then the footsteps get closer then they stop.  Then someone yells his name. Aries!

I wake up sweating immensely. Tears splash out of my eyes.  I look up and see Shaun sitting in the chair asleep; he wakes up from the slight scream that escapes my lips.  What is happening to me? That nightmare had went away, I willed it away, I had told myself only good memories and now it was back haunting me.

"Are you all right", he asks as he rushes over to bedside and I put my arms around him.

Don't let me go.  I am shaking, He could feel my body vibrate on his and you can see the concern in his eyes.

"I won't", he says, holding me as hard as he can.  My trembling stops after a few minutes.  He looks at me, smiles and kisses me.  His breath is so sweet and calming, reminding me of my first taste of chocolate as a child. In this moment it was like I have never been kissed by him, he is my valium.

"I want you come stay with me."

I can't.

"You can't go back there."

I know but I can't live with you.

"I know we've only known each other for a minute but I do love you and besides it doesn't have to be forever just until you find a place if that's what you want."

Don't say that.

"Say what?"

That you love me, everyone that loves me dies.  He looks at me with perplexed eyes, wondering about the words that have just passed my lips. I feel my pulse begin to race and my eyes starting to water as my heart beat as if it is about to detonate. He kisses me, he pulls away, takes my hand and kisses me again, looks directly in my light brown eyes.

"Having a day to love you is the best damn thing anyone could ever hope for. Let me have the rest of my life." He raises his hand and wipes my tears. They stop. My heart slows down yet my pulse continues to race. I agree to move in with him.

Michael and Kim arrange for my belongings to be moved out, placing most of my things in storage.  They bring my clothes to

Shaun's place which I haven't left for five days. The police stop by to do a final wrap up and I also get a visit from a Shaun's attorney, Carl Franklin.  He has an envelope for me. I open the envelope, inside are some legal documents and a letter, I open the letter first.

> *Dear Gabe,*
> *I wanted to write you and tell you how important you are to me.  I have made choices over that time that not only affected my life but also yours. For any pain that I have caused you, I sincerely apologize but from what I hear you are doing well now and have grown up to be the man I can be proud of and a man I would want my son to learn from.  A couple of months ago me and Sara decided to make a will and the most important part was who did we want raising our son if something happen to us. Sara knows we were are friends, I have always told her we were like family.  I could not go any further than that, which is my burden not hers. So I have decided and Sara has agreed that our son should be raised by not only the man I most admire, respect but the one that I trust and love, that is you. I know this is a lot to ask for but I am sure you can live up to that challenge of raising a black man, one that I know will be proud and one that we can be proud of.  It will not be easy but I ask you to honor me by accepting this responsibility. Please let me share the one gift, we could not share together, with you, if something happens to us.*
>
> *Love always,*
> *Simon*

I look at the attorney and I think this is some joke.
"Do you understand what he is asking?"
Yes, but this has to be some joke.
"No, he was very sure about this detail."
Where is Brian now?
"He's at a foster home until we could take care of this custody situation."
"You don't have to do this", Shaun says.
If I can't do this.

"Then your brother and sister in law have a decision to make.  Let me just say Simon was adamant that it was you, that kind of trust and faith is very rare."

Do I have to decide now?

"No, but he's in a foster home and his case comes in front of family court judge in the morning."

I'll be there, call me with the details. Carl leaves and Shaun and I are alone.

"This wasn't your fault."

I know that.

"So really think about this, this kid would change your whole life."

You don't think I know that. What is it?

"He was in your house and naked."

You want to know why he was there.

"I trust you."

Do you?

"Yes, I do but I wouldn't be human if I didn't want to know why he was there.  You loved this guy, he's killed by his wife but ass naked in your house, I guess I'm curious."

I love you.

"That's not an answer."

He needed a place to stay; he'd left Sara for good. A part of me will always love him but there was nothing going on, he'd just got of the shower when she came to the door. I had given up on Shaun and although he would always be a part of my soul, I knew he could never be a part of my life.

"Even if he was done with her?"

Even if. Do you doubt what I feel for you?

"Damn it Gabriel, I don't doubt it but you can't doubt it either."

So I count on you.

"Always."

I want to honor his request and take custody of Brian. I want to raise him.

"How will you explain to him about his parents."

I'll tell him the truth.

"Truth is a dangerous thing. Is this out of guilt."

No, I love that little boy, this is what's right.

"Then I'll be right by your side. Come here." Shaun pulls me to him and we embrace. No one every said life was easy but damn I've had enough heartache for two life times.  This is the moment I turn some of my sadness into joy for someone else.

The next morning we make our way down to the family court for the hearing. I can tell Shaun is just as nervous as I am. As we walk into the building, through sets of double doors, my heart begin to race as we scan the room.  An old lady sits in chair filling out a form with two little girls, on who is crying uncontrollably but barely making a sound. There is a loud buzz sound and Brian comes out with an elderly black lady in a maroon dress and another Carl carrying a briefcase. Brian races across the room and jumps up in my arms.

"Uncle Gabe", he yells, "are you here to take me home?"

Why yes I am.

"They told me momma and daddy are gone to heaven."

I know B, that's why I am here. Do you want to come live with me?

"Yes."

I was hoping you would say that.

"Go back with Ms. Green Brian, I need to talk to your Uncle Gabe." Brian jumps out my arms and makes his way over to the lady.

What's wrong?

"Nothing, I just need to go over a few things."

All right.

"First we'll be asking for temporary custody and the start of the adoption process which won't be completed for over a year. They'll visit your home multiple times during this upcoming year.  I hear you are staying at Shaun's' place."

Yes.

"Find your own place quickly. The judge will have lost of questions and he has gone over police reports, so it might get personal and this won't be easy." I look at Carl as he explains all the obstacles and nuances of the hearing.  He stood just slightly taller than me. His head is a bit wide but he has a permanent smile attached to his face. He exudes confidence and his voice rings of intelligence and assurance. His gestures are strong and powerful. He tells me exactly what he needs me to say and he leads us into the courtroom. As I walk next to Shaun my insides are spinning out of control. I begin to have doubts about raising Brian. What if I couldn't give him all the love and affection he would need. What if the knowledge of the reasons and way his parents died made him resent me, even hate me. I look over at Shaun and he must sense my fears, he reaches down and squeezes my hand.

The courtroom is cold and icy.  The wooden benches and emptiness of the room is overwhelming. Brian sits next to the lady and Shaun and I sit up in front with Carl. The judge enters and the courtroom is called in session by the bailiff. I turn to see people from DCFS sitting at the other table.  The Judge starts off by saying that he has doubts about this arrangement considering the circumstances but since all parties think this is a functional situation he would allow me temporary custody but assured me that this case will be monitored heavily and a decision will be made on the adoption after a year of placement in my home. As the judge stands to leave the room I turn to Brian and he looks up at me.
"Do I get to go home with you Uncle Gabe?"
You sure do.  His face lit up and the look in his eyes lifted some of the weight off of my heart. I grab for his hand and we walk out of the courtroom. In some ways I need Brian more than he needs me. I need him to rebuild my heart.  This is a restructure process and all the worries and tears that had overtaken me have vanished.  I have put aside all my pain and sorrow and focused on this little boy. I have grieved to a point where I had lost sight of anything that may have lain before me. I couldn't save Simon, or Aries but I can save Brian, matter of fact it is him who is saving me. That is the truth, this boy is saving me.

Brian and I find a house in the near south side of Chicago, off State and Balbo. It was very reasonable and the neighborhood had steadily improved over the years. It is easier access to work and closer to Shaun, who is now only five minutes away. Brian loves his new room which Shaun had more fun decorating than I did. We've been here for about four days and Brian has spent a lot of time playing in it that I am beginning to worry that he is going inward. Brian walks in to the living room where I am doing research and sits next to me. I place my laptop on the table and turn to him.
What's wrong champ?

"What happen to my mommy and daddy?" I look into this child's eyes and I am almost moved to tears. I should have prepared myself to answer this question.

What do you want to know?

"Did they go to heaven or hell?" I smile, I want to laugh. To heaven of course, I say with a sigh of relief. He smiles as I tell him:

Your parents are now angels and they will be watching over you and protecting the both of us. Every time you want to talk to them, they are right here in your heart. I pointed to his heart then grabbed him and start tickling him and he erupts in laughter. Brian returns to the vivacious little boy that he was when I first met him. I know one day that he will come back and have more in-depth questions, so I must begin preparing for that day. For now I will enjoy having him in my life and creating a secure family for him and myself.

The months begin to fly by, February, March, April, May, June and school is ending. Over five months with Brian and I have planned a vacation with Shaun to Seattle. It is a week away, when the doorbell rings. I open it and Shaun stands and I think nothing over it since he we have dinner plans and some special party planning to do for Brian's birthday. He comes in and sits down on the couch looking as if the world has just taken a nose dive on all around him

What's wrong?

"I was traded this afternoon."

Where to, I ask trying not to let him see the unhappiness that I feel.

"To Dallas."

I see. What does that mean?

"I'll be moving there."

What does that mean for us?

"I want you and Brian to come with me." I look at him. There is no doubt in my mind that I would do that if it was only me, but it just isn't possible or reasonable. I can't unsettle my life definitely not Brian's life. I stare at Shaun, his eyes, I could see the fear and concern in his eyes.

I can't do that, if it was only me, I might consider going with you but I can't do that to Brian. He's just now starting to feel comfortable. I can't uproot him, he has to come first and besides the adoption isn't final.

"Do you love me?"

Of course I do but that really isn't the question is it?

"At least think about it."

There is no need Shaun. Maybe we can do a long distance relationship, I do love you but I can't move with you.

"Maybe you don't love me enough."

How can you say that to me? His words struck my heart like a million daggers.

"I'm sorry that was unfair.  Maybe we can make it work, long distance."

I want it to.  So when do you leave?

"In a week."

Then let's make this the best week.  I hug him and then we leave to pick up Brian from camp.

We pick up Brian and tell him about Shaun's move. He is unhappy but I assure him that we will see Shaun all the time. That seems to settle him down and for me his comfort, comforts my own fears. We drive to the restaurant, you know the one with the big rat out front, where a kid can be a kid and Brian fills us in all his adventures at camp. It is exciting watching Brian run around with twenty or so children so involved in their play. Shaun of course took all of the attention from the parents; the fathers especially flock to him.  I sit and watch in awe at his charisma.

On the car ride home I think we are all tired and overwhelmed by such a full day.  Shaun drives and Brian sings all the way home. Shaun stares out of the window not saying a word; I know what this silence means. Brian stops singing and turns to me.

"I miss them."

Me too, I talk to them all the time.

"What do they say?"

For you not to worry about them, they're fine.

"When you talk them again, will you tell them I love them?"

You can tell them that, remember they are always with you.

"I try but I don't hear them."

Next time just listen really carefully, they'll talk right back.

"I'll try."

And I'll let them know you are listening for them. Brian lays down on the back sit I am sure he must be tired from his

long day and soon he is asleep but not soundly at all.  Shaun
reaches over and takes my hand.  I lean over and kiss him.

July has come and I am at the airport with Shaun.  We keep
reassuring each other that we will be fine.  I'm not sure either one
of us believed that.  As much as I believe in what we feel, it still
doesn't comfort me. As I stand against the wall, Shaun sits in
front of me.  I stare at him but he doesn't turn to look at me.  He
stares straight ahead out of the airport window. Flight 124 to
Dallas is now boarding is the announcement that blares over the
intercom. My eyes begin to ache. A tear drop forms in the
crevice of eye, my hand moves up to wipe it away.  Shaun
stands and turns to me.  He picks up my hand and holds it in
both of his.  I look at the way his hands completely engulfs min.  I
like the way it feels when he touches me.  Las night he had
touch every inch of my body and my body aches with that
memory.  I look up at him.
        "Don't, it's not goodbye," he says, but it is, for all intent
and purpose.  Shaun is walking directly out of my life as
unexpectedly as he walked into it. Sure we might see each other
but not the way we should.  Someone once said absence makes
the heart grow fonder, the truth is that only if you really don't care
about a person do you care about them when they're gone, that
way you can have them live up to your dreams.
        "Come here," he says, yanking me into him.  We stand so
close that his breath warms the hair on my upper lips. I want to
kiss him but hug is all I can muster.
        I love you, I say as I feel my hold grow tighter around his
body.
        "I love you too and nothing will ever change that."  I let go
of him, looking up at him, knowing that this was one of the
hardest things I will do. When you find love, you have to hold on
to it.  You can't let go.  You can never leave the side of the one
you love because there is always someone waiting to take your
place.  I had let him in and now I can't let him go.

As he walks through the terminal door, he turns and waves to
me.  He blows me a kiss and I manage a smile.  I had to leave
him with a smile not anger, pain and disappointment at what life
was once again throwing my way.  Chaka Kahn said it best,
*"Through the fire, to the limits"*, that's exactly where we are
constantly being pushed, shoved and forced to our limits. As the

doors close I stand in the window for fifteen minutes until the place begins it's take off.  I don't know why I want to watch him fly away. Maybe I am hoping he would pull a Whitney Houston moment from the Body Guard and jump off the place and run back into my arms. It's funny how when you're in love, scenes from movies take on a more intense, even mesmerizing feeling when you desire them to happen to you.  I do realize this isn't a movie, it is my life and unfortunately my life is written more by a tragic German writer of the twenties not the romantic hacks of Hollywood.  If I believe in any one thing, I believe in love.

Driving back from the airport, I wonder what he is thinking at this moment.  Am I on his mind?  Is he telling the person next to him he has left his heart in Chicago, or is he already picking out a new love? Damn I almost hit the car but fortunately, I miss.  I know I could not go into a depression over this; after all I do have a child to take care of.  So as I turn into Michaels' driveway to pick up Brian, I have to put on a smile, I have to let the pain settle for a moment. I have focus on the love. It's so damn easy to say but not so easy to accomplish.  People write great songs about love but do they really understand them, most likely not. Love is the one thing you can be certain to let you down and pick you up.  Love is certain to be uncertain.

As I sit on the couch in the living room, listening to some Ani Dfranco, I started listening to her on a visit to California one summer some six years ago.  As her song 32 flavors play out of my I-pod, Brian walks into the living room.  He comes and sits next to me and begins to listen with me.
     "Why are you so sad?"
     Why do you think I'm sad?
     "Your eyes, they're red.  You shouldn't cry he's only in Texas."
     I know.
     "Besides, he's always here. In here," he says pointing at my chest.
     You know, you're right and I squeeze him tightly.  I begin to tickle him and he laughs and laughs. Come on, I tell him, it's time for bed.  I pick him up and sit him on y shoulders and walk him to his room. I lay beside him after he changes and he reads me a story from his favorite book, Little Ninja Boys. He soon falls asleep and I rub his head thinking how different my life is

becoming now that he was the most important part.  My life was settling down.  Brian had fulfilled my dream of being a father, although it wasn't even close to the way I had imagined.

At the office, I work at my desk, trying not to remember all the pain I have experienced over the course of the last few weeks. Shaun had been missing in action for a while.  I have only seen him twice in the last month, yes I speak to him every day but it is not quite the same. Reggie enters the room and looks and smiles at me. I return the smile and continue to work. I was putting on the finishing touches for my article about the influx of blacks into the Republican Party. I had interview JC Watts, although I really don't care much for him and I was not talking about his politics. American is not the same country it was twenty years or two years ago. Reggie walks over to me and I look up at him.

What's up?
"I wanted to know if you had lunch yet? If not my treat."
I'm pretty busy.
Come on, you need a break, you work so damn hard."
Oh you think so?
"I know so."
All right, where are we going?
"Bazelles, off North and Wells, pretty good Cajun food."
Give me ten minutes to wrap this up.
"Ten minutes", he says as he walks back to his desk and begins to work. I finish up my article and start to spell check on my computer. I wrap up and look up and Reggie is standing putting on his sweater.  He looks over at me and I stand grab my keys and we head out the door.

The food is good. The shrimp gumbo, which I have and the Jambalaya, which Reggie has, just water in your mouth. We drink some red wine and Reggie keeps me engulfed in good conversation. We talk about raising young boys and I finally have the chance of sharing my fears with someone who understands. As the lunch progresses I see a Reggie I had not seen before. Yes, he has always been cute, charming and cordial but he is open and receptive. The more we talk, the more my desire rises for him. I smile at his jokes, then I feel his hand land on mine, I look down and then back up into his gray eyes.
You didn't have Nadine with you over the holidays?

"She was with mom and dad," he says without moving his hand, so I withdraw mine.  I want to leave it there but I can't. Maybe it is the alcohol or maybe it is confusion.

Why didn't she stay home with her husband and little boy? He laughs a hearty laugh which makes me self-conscious.

She's not my wife, she's my sister.

Really?

"Yes, really. I haven't dated a woman in eleven years.

I'm surprise; you seem like a good catch.

"You're serious.  It's been by choice Gabriel, I'm gay."

Oh.

"Over the past two years, I've seen you with Simon, Shaun and yes Peter, don't you think it's time for you to be with someone who is ready to be with you completely and deeply."

Shaun loves me and I love him, so what do you know about my life.

"I know eventually Shaun will fail you too."

So what, you're throwing your hat into the ring.

"No, I'm tossing my heart in the ring. Those others just aren't the man who can be your rock and hold you when you feel heartache, they aren't the men who will lift you up and encourage you to take risks, and they won't understand true, deep love." I look at him and can't decide whether to knock the shit out of him or lean into his chest and breathe freely.

I love Shaun.

"You have a different choice now."

At home I sit reading while Brian sits on the floor doing his homework. I couldn't concentrate, Shaun was flying home tomorrow to convince me to move to Dallas with him and I have taken the day off to spend with him. I am so excited about seeing him but Reggie was consuming my soul.

"Daddy can you help me with math homework?"

What did you call me?

"I'm sorry."

For what?

"I shouldn't call you daddy."

No, if you want to, that's fine, I was just surprised. My eyes are aching now, I never want him to forget or replace Simon but I want us both to heal. This meant to me he had begun to trust me. I lay my begin to look down and kneel down next to him and lay flat on my stomach.  We look over the problems and begin to work them out.  I rub his head and he looks up at me and he smiles. He is my bright young man, although I can't take credit for that, I am still extremely proud.  The phone rings.

Hello.

"Hey it's Reggie, did I wake you?"

No.

"I want to apologize for lunch.  Maybe we can try to b friends."

Is that possible?

"We can try.  Since the kids are out of school on Tuesday, why don't we take them to the zoo, it'll be fun."

I think Brian would like that.

"Good, I'll call you on Monday.  Goodnight."

Goodnight.


As I tuck Brian into bed and read to him "The Rise of a Great Empire", he listens with intent ears and quickly dozes off.  I watch him resting so peacefully, I notice the way his lips move and quiver ever so slightly as he sleeps. I think of all the things that I want in my life and although maybe not the way I would have preferred I am getting them all.


I walk into my bedroom and turn on the radio and immediately Whitney Houston voice begin to fill the air, *I believe in you and me, I believe that we will be in love eternally*. I picked up the phone and dial Shaun's number.

"Hello."

Hello is Shaun there?

"No, he went to Chicago for the weekend."

Who am I speaking with?

"Bradley, I'm house sitting for him."

Thanks. As I sat down the phone, I begin to wonder why had he hadn't call to tell me he was leaving early.  I want to know when was he going to tell me Bradley was in Dallas and that he was staying at his house. As I contemplate this my buzzer sounds. I rush down the hall and push the intercom.

Yes.

"It's Shaun."

Come on up.  I buzz him in through the front door and walk down to the front door and look in the mirror.  I wipe the paste out of the corner of my eyes and wetting my lips as I head to the door.  I open the door and he stands there with his suitcase, the sight of him almost takes my breath away, I smile and he smiles.

"You're not surprised?"

No.

"You called, no fair."

Didn't mean to ruin the surprise. Shaun enters, close the door and I pull him into my body and we kiss.  The excitement of feeling his lips on mine is a little overwhelming. My heart is pulsing with intensity and passion and I know that all those lonely nights without him are about to be taken care of.

"Where's Brian?"

Sleep.

"We should head to bed too."

You're not going to tell me why Bradley is at your house.

"He was just traded and needed a place to stay for a minute."

What Dallas closed all the hotels?

"Are you jealous?"

No, irritated is more like it. How could you not tell me?

"I didn't want it to become an issue. There is nothing going on between me and him."

How long is that going to last. He still loves you.

"Brad never loved me, he only loved the sex."

For some there is no difference.

"For me there is, I love only you", he leans in and kisses me "Can we go to bed so I can show you how much it's been almost two months."

All I am is your Chicago sex stop.

Then let's get to it then. I begin to walk to the room and he grabs hold of my waist and I led him to our bedroom. My body is ablaze with the anticipation of what is about to come.


As I lay in bed, Shaun is in the kitchen getting us something to drink. The bedroom door is pushed open and Brian walks in and jumps in bed with me.

"Someone is in the kitchen."

It's Uncle Shaun. Shaun enters with two glasses of juice, wearing his red gym shorts; Brian jumps out of bed and wraps his arms around his waist. Shaun carries him on waist back to the bed as I turn on the television. The three of us lay in bed watching a late night movie on A&E.  It is Orson Welles Lady from Shanghai.  We watch for a while until Brian returns to slumber land and Shaun carries him back to his room and returns to my side.  He hops back into bed and I lean onto his chest.  He strokes my head and I feel at ease.

"Are we a family?"

Yes, I think so, I want us to be.

"Then move to Dallas."

You mean in a year or two?

"No, I mean now."

I can't, my job, I can't uproot Brian.

"He wants us to be together."

So do I, but I can't move now.

"So what happens to us?"

We survive, we love each other.

"Is that enough? People love each other all the time and they always end up apart.  I don't want that for us.  It took me long enough to find you."

I love you and I would never do anything to lose you.

"I love you."

I know.  We begin to kiss and all the other things mattered less.  We are together and that was the cure for any problems that were there at least for now. Love may not solve all our problems but it sure is a nice friend to have along for the ride.

The entire weekend we were a family. Exactly the one I had imagined so many years ago. The players were different and so were the circumstances but my dream of having a family had come true. Hanging out with Shaun is a little different then say having a doctor by your side.  Not many people would recognize the doctor or come up and ask for an autograph. Brian actually thought it was exciting. It made him feel special, and he is right it is special. Shaun was gracious in all that he did, he had an ego but it just wasn't about being an athlete. After a group of two twenty something females, decided they needed pictures and more of his time, Shaun comes over to where Brian and I are sitting and slides next to me. He stares at me, smiling with his eyes and looks away. He looks at me like so often and I still never can quite tell what he is thinking. When he looks at me again I feel safe, I feel that for the first time in a long time I can let the shell around my heart crack. He moves his lips and tells me with soundless words, I love you. I smile and wink he laughs and we leave.

It is night time and I sit looking out of the window, reach over to the night stand and pull out a pack of cigarettes that have been in there for over six months.  The room is quiet, the silence echoes inside me.  I don't know what to think.  To say my life has been complicated would be an understatement. It also seems every time I begin to feel normalcy of just plan damn hope something steps in and tears that page completely out of my book. I am a strong man that I am sure of others might not recover from one of these tragic events but I am here, stronger than ever. Can I be happy or will fate waltz up another slow dance of despair and take out once again. I didn't hear Shaun get up from the bed, he slides up behind me takes the cigarette from my hand and tosses out the window. When he wraps his hands around me I lean into him grabbing at his elbows. I feel his manhood stiffening underneath me, he smiles an expression in his eyes a look I had become familiar with. We did not speak as the night air took over us. This had become a regular scene for us, just enjoying each other without words. Once again I felt secure with him, in these moments, in this moment I was aware that I had once again found love and the tear rolled down my cheek.

It's Monday Brian and I driving Shaun to the airport.  We stand in the foyer holding each other, not wanting to let go.  I can't let him go but I know I must. He never brought up the move again but I know it is on his mind and I am leaning toward making the big step. We get in the car and he plays with Brian and cracks jokes as I drive in silence. At the airport we say our goodbyes and Shaun goes through the terminal and we head back to the car. I drop Brian off at school and head to work. I have a meeting with Laurence Phelps a managing editor at a local paper he is interested in me working for them. I am not ready to leave CONURBATION but I agreed to meet with him today. I make my way up into the Chicago building and stop at the receptionist on the fourteenth floor; she has me take a seat and calls back. A few minutes later she calls for me and I stand and I am greeted by a man about five eleven, reaching his hand out towards me, I grab his hand.

   "I'm Laurence Phelps", he says.

   Good to meet you.  He his younger than I was expecting, he looks early thirties but I know by his resume he is at least in his mid-forties. His short hair is perfectly tampered around his head. His ears are equally aligned and a nose that is shaped and placed with precise on his face. His picture perfect eyebrows and eyelashes are colored and toned to complete his mocha skin. His lips are medium sized and when he smiles his teeth glare from the sunlight.

"Let's go into my office". He turns and I follow watching his toned body, reacting through his tailored suit, which hugs his ass in just the right amount of thickness. We sit in his office and I notice the manicured hands and the wedding ring that clings to his hand.  Laurence begins to talk to me about the job and how I was the only name on this job list. He explained to me the freedom I would have on the job.  I listen with tentative ears, waiting for the right words that would either make me accept the job or turn it down flatly. I heard them when said he understands I have a little boy and with them family was a priority and that he had no conflicts with me freelancing for other outlets as long as they were not competitors. I want to take job now, on the spot but I tell him I need a couple of days to think about and talk it over with my family.

I decide to walk back to office, which is only a few blocks away. Downtown Chicago is a colorful city. The people seem to be oblivious to anyone around them, self-involved. All dressed in the power suits and ties trying to mask their unhappiness, I think we are taught from an early age to keep a distance from anything real and that is why so many of us are so unhappy. If you make eye contact with anyone they turn as if some heavy force has just slapped their face. I make a stop at the drug house, I mean Starbucks to pick up my triple soy latte.  As I wait for my drink I feel a pair of eyes on me.  I look out of the corner of my eyes and there stands a Latino man. He is dressed in a light gray suit with a soft gray tie and pink tie.  He is about six feet take, curly hair, and black.  His eyes are glimmering green.  His broad eyebrows enhance the light in his eyes to mere perfection; it has to be the sunlight. A finely trimmed mustache and goatee lines his face and make his lips, which are red and thick as his tongue run gently across them.  I look back up at his eyes and he smiles. No Gabe, I keep thinking, do not give off that interested look. You know the one where you smile and kind of tilt your head just enough to invite him over and let him know you have seen him. I smile and tilt anyway. I get my drink and walk over to the condiment counter and place three packs of Splenda in my Grande drink.  He moves beside me and causally looks over to me.

"Excuse me", he says as he leans across me arm for the regular sugar.

No problem, I say as I look up at him, only to find myself smiling.

"I just had to have my second cup", the conversation has began and I have two choices, I can continue or I can walk away.

I hear you, I'm Gabriel.

"Nelson," he says with a nice slight accent rolling off his lips with the last word.  I stare up into his eyes.  I guess I should feel a little guilt but it is just flirting. We exit the coffee house and begin walking westward down Harrison.  Nelson it turns out is a broker for the Chicago exchange. He is twenty eight single with no kids.  He lives in Wicker Park.  We get to m office and I stop and he stands in front of me.

This is me. Thanks for the conversation.

"Here is my number", he says as he takes out a pen and writes it on the back of his business card. I take it and place it in my wallet.

I know you can't give out yours. I look up in his eyes and he smiles, then turns down Harrison and going east.  I stand for a minute and watch him leave, he turns back once and I then enter the office complex and go inside. I would never cheat on Shaun but having that guy take time to flirt with me did make me feel really good. Nothing's wrong with a little harmless flirting.

I walked out of the elevator into the office and to my desk.  I spot a message in the middle of my desk. It was from Wilson, he left me his cell phone number.  I pick up the phone and dial.  Wilson answers and sounds tired.  He asks me to meet him at the corner of Harrison and Michigan, so I quickly make my way out of the office.  I had never heard him sound so low.  He rings of pain and confusion.  I try to figure out could be bothering him but nothing comes to mind so I just decide to wait and find out from the source. As I reach the corner, I spot Wilson standing alone, pacing in a five step interval.  I walk up to him and reach out to shake his hand he engulfs min with both of his, releases it and begins to walk, I jog up to catch up with him.  We walk through Grant Park for several minutes without saying a word.  Finally he sits down on a bench. I sit next to him and try to read his face to no avail.

"I didn't know who else to call.  I know you probably aren't the best choice but I couldn't think of anyone else I wanted to talk to, not about this." Wilson says without changing his glare from the sidewalk. Then there was silence again.  Then he looks up at me.

What is it?

"My wife, Lora, she's having an affair."

What?

"My daughters mention this guy a month ago but when I heard them mention him again my alarms starting getting louder. I knew something was wrong but she always said it was fine. So I came home early on Thursday and I saw him leaving the house. Friday I followed her and she met him for lunch. She kissed him."

Maybe it was just a kiss.

"You don't kiss another mans' wife like that."

Did you ask her?

"Yes, she denied it at first, but I told her I saw her and she starts crying and she admits it. I should have seen this. The sad thing about the boy can't be more than twenty five. How could she do this to me, I have loved this woman and not once have I betrayed her."

What are you going to do?

"I don't know." I took out my cell phone and asked Kim to pick up Brian and I call Reggie and cancel the boys play date. Wilson and I go back to my place; we sit on my couch and talk about Lora and his love for her. He had given up so much of himself for the love he felt for her. He wanted the American dream and for a long time he had just that but the tears that slowing glides down his cheek told of the American nightmare. When you lose something you hold dear nothing can bring that back even it wasn't real to begin with.

Can you forgive her?

"I don't know.  I wasn't enough for her, who knows if I ever will be?"

You need to talk to her; betrayal is not always the end.

"Come on Gabe, could you?"

I did, with Aries. We got through it and we would have survived.

"Is love really worth, I've been in love twice, the first time I was so scared I purposely destroyed it and this time I was burned. Maybe I am just not meant for this."

That's just damn silly. As clichéd as it might sound love is a gift that everyone can have. It may not be perfect or last for eternity but what part you can hold of it you should never regret it.  The phone rings and it is Brian, he's called to say goodnight. He tells me about his day. As I say goodnight to my son, the line buzzes and I click over it is Reggie.

"Things all right?"

Had to help a friend.

"Is he all right?"

He will be.

"Call me if you need anything."

Thanks Reggie I will, I talk to you tomorrow. I hang up the phone and Wilson looks at me.

"Reggie huh?"

We're friends, nothing else. He smiles and I show him where he can sleep tonight and I head to my bed to get some much needed rest.


As I lay in bed, I think back to my life before Aries, with him and after him. I realize how blessed I am. I truly understand Wilsons' pain, I had survived it myself/ Love was important but it can be damn messy and make you feel like it's just not worth it. Nights like tonight, I try to stay awake because emotions brings back thoughts of Aries and the image that is always the strongest is the blood gushing from his body as he dies in my arms.  Wilson enters the room and the clock reads one thirty.

What's wrong?

"I don't want to be alone." I stare at him for a few seconds and raise my sheet and he crawls in bed next to me. I wrap my arms around his body; his warmth is still fresh in my memories. Wilson has always been the standard for ruggedness for me. He was sexy and the picture of manliness. Tonight he is wounded and vulnerable and I was allowing him to use me as his band aid. He places his fingers through mine and pulls my hand into his cheek.  I could feel his heart beating hundreds of beats per minutes and mine begin to keep pace. I soon fall asleep and I know what I am doing. I am comforting a friend, when a friend goes though the fires of life, they don't need to have them put out because those fires are what make us who we are. What they need is for someone to be there to help them walk, stand tall and keep moving, because life is too damn special for us to get burned up by those moments of not giving a damn.

When I wake up I feel a sense of calm.  I look beside me Wilson is still sound asleep. It was kind of nice being here next to him.  It is still a little weird becoming friends to someone I had spent so many passionate nights, sweating to Barry White. I wanted to take away his pain, to have him feel good once again, but I can't do that, I just had to let him go where all his pain takes him. I crawl out of bed and head into the shower.  The warm water hits my body with such great force that I almost fall down.  After a few seconds, it feels so nice against my skin, massaging out all the sexual tension that I had acquired last night.

After Wilson wakes up he borrows a shirt so he could go to work and I head into the office myself. I don't get much work done, my mind isn't here. I keep thinking about Shaun and how I want to be with him but I can't.  Then it hit me I could be in Dallas Friday night. So I call Shaun and tell him that I am coming to see him, he is excited. He asks me if I have made a choice and I tell him I have.

I have lunch with Reggie, I like talking to him. We take a walk after lunch and day gets better.  I love Shaun but I can't help but feel a twinge of guilt because I know this moment that I am sharing with Reggie is wrong. It is wrong because I am enjoying it too much and the attraction is here and it is not one sided. Is this connection that we both share wrong?  After work we go pick up Brian and then Reggie's son RJ.  We take them to a seven o'clock showing of the Rocket Man, the boys love the movie. They talk about becoming astronauts, we both hope they won't, but boys will be boys.  At the pizza place afterwards, we watch the boys play together. I am happy that Brian was so happy.  He and RJ are getting alone great; he even asks if he can stay over at Reggie's house.  I wasn't sure about tonight but it Reggie had already agreed for the one weekend so what would one more night matter.

We went to my house to pick up a few things for Brian. I realized that I had missed a few calls on my phone and I listened to the messages, the first from Shaun saying to call him when I get back from Brian play date and another from Laurence Phelps saying he needed to see me first thing in the morning.  The last message was from Wilson asking if I could put him up for one more night.  Then it was Kim,

Gabe, it's Kim, your father had a heart attack, and he's at University of Chicago. I hope you get this message soon." I didn't know what to feel but I knew I should feel something.  I should feel fear but I don't think I feel that. I walk out into the dining room where RJ and Brian are chasing each other and Reggie looks up at me.

"What's wrong?"

My father, he's had a heart attack.

"What do you need me to do?"

Take Brian.

"Do you want me to drive you to the hospital?"

No, I think I can manage. I had him Brian's bag and they leave. I sit down on my couch.  I didn't know what I should do. The doorbell rings and Wilson stand there.

"What's wrong?"

It's my father, he's at the hospital.

"I'll go with you."

No, you stay here, I'll go. I leave the house and head down to the medical center.

As I enter the hospital I stop at the desk and tell them I am looking for Samuel Richards.  The lady looks him up and tells me he's in ICU. As I enter the elevator to head up I felt my heart stop if only for a moment. What if he was dead and we never got a chance to amend for those hurtful words we had said to one another.  Deep inside I had been sure that we would have time and we would have a chance to make things right. Exiting the elevator I see Kim sitting in chair and Michael leaning onto her shoulder.  I walk up to them and Michael stands and covers me with his body, this is one of the few vulnerable moments I can remember with my brother. He has always been the picture of strength for me.  I must admit it always makes me stand back and realize that sometimes he needs me to be strong for him.

I call Shaun and tell him I'm not going to make it to Dallas, he says he'll come but I tell him not to make the trip. Soon the doctor tells us we can go in that he's awake but needs his rest. I tell my mother and Michael I'll wait out here in the waiting area but Michael insists I come in; my mother remains quiet, like she has for the last three hours. It is hard to see the man in the bed when he does not resemble the man who uses to sing old Motown tunes to us. He would make my mother melt like an old school girl. Those moments seemed so perfect who know they would all disappear just as easily as they had come. I approach his bed and he reaches out his hand to take mine.  At this moment all the pain all the anger, all the frustration disappear and I lean down and whisper to him,

I love you dad. For a moment I can see the love in his eyes, I see the man who use to sit by my bed a read to me every night until I was ten and then who use to listen to me read to him until I was thirteen every night. I see love in his eyes and I am once again at peace. His lips begin to move and the grip on my hand tightens, so I lean down to him.

"You are the biggest disappointment of my life," he says slicing through me as smoothly as a knife through water. I yank my hand away and walk out of the room. Michael follows me out.

"Gabe, stop"

There's nothing else to say. If nothing else I am sure he meant those words.

"Gabe, he's dying."

Yeah, I know at least God is getting something right.

"Don't say anything you will regret."

You mean like telling your son that he is the biggest disappointment of your life. Michael, you go back to him, I am fine, I really am. That man in there has been dead to me for so long that this right here, this moment means very little.

"You love him and he loves you, I know that."

At one time you might have been right but the love is gone and I still have time to catch my plane, so I'll see you in a few days. I turn and begin walking down the hall. I had allowed my heart to be reopened and he stuck a sword in it. I needed Shaun; I needed him to hold me.


Here I am sitting on the plane; I couldn't reach Shaun to tell him that plans had changed. I needed this weekend to rejuvenate and make sure that what my father had done don't dig me any deeper in the pain of my soul. Watching the plane land on the runway, I was able to see the skyline of Dallas, it was beautiful at night. Once I reached the baggage claim, I make another attempt to call Shaun but he still did not answer. I have keys so I am not worried he probably just went out to get something to eat I think to myself. I grab a cab and make my way to his apartment. The ride is uneventful.

I enter Shaun's apartment and sit my bags down, I notice cold food on the counter along with two empty bottles of wine. I hear the faint sound of music coming from the back so I make my way toward the bedroom. As I approach the music gets louder and my heart beats gets heavier. I walk to door and open it and there in bed lies Bradley all 6 feet five inches of him, on his stomach. I back up and my eyes begin to water, my heart stopped at that moment. My soul has left my body. The bathroom door opens and Shaun comes out wrapped in a towel.

 "Gabriel." I walk right past him, head to the front, to reach my bags.

 "Wait let me explain."

I don't think you need to.

 "Yes I do, I'm sorry."

I have to go.

 "He came over and we got to drinking…"

…Just stop. You and Bradley, damn!

 "It was a mistake, I love you."

What the fuck does love have to do with this? I trusted you, I love you.

 "I'm so sorry."

I have to go.

 "Please Gabriel, don't leave, not like this. This was not supposed to happen."

 Which part fucking him or getting caught?

 "Neither one. It was a mistake and it meant nothing."

 Is that supposed to make this any better? Goodbye Shaun. I turn pick up my bags and exit out of the front door with my heart rattling around in my body in a million tiny pieces.

The hotel room is quiet, the temperature is just right. I can't sleep all night. I lie awake in my bed, I can't cry, I can't do anything and my mind won't quit wondering how did I get to this point. How did I lose everything, when everything seemed worth the fight? The sun rose quickly around me, I did not know what to do. I was headed back home more devastated then when I arrived. No music could heal my soul at this point, I just wanted to melt away in the bed but I had to get back to my son. I was brought from my sleep by a knock at the door. I rise from the bed, heart still in pieces and I look through the peephole. There he stands the object of my depression. I open the door.

Why are you here?

"I couldn't sleep all night."

Well lucky for you your bed is used for other things,

"Damn it, I made a mistake."

How many times did you make that same mistake?

"It was once."

How am I to believe that?

"Because you know I love you, I was stupid, but the one thing I never stopped doing was loving you."

It's that just damn great, you love me so much that you fuck another dude.

"You want me to move back quit, give it all up."

It doesn't matter dude, it doesn't fucking matter, everything I felt for you I left at your front door.

"So that's it?"

Yes, it is. The good thing for you is that you have someone waiting to pick up right where they left off at last night.

"You think it's that easy?"

What is not easy is having your father tell you that you are his biggest mistake the same night you walk in on the person you love finish screwing someone else. But you know niggas are all the same. Get the fuck out my room so I can get ready to leave this town. Shaun reaches for me and I pull away, he turns and closes the door behind him and I turn and sit on the couch and for the first time I begin to cry. All the tears, all the pain came rushing out and at this moment I don't know if they ever would stop.

I enter my apartment and turn on my radio and listen to the tunes blare out into the air. I cannot listen to anything that is upbeat but I do try, I end of settling on some mellow music. Music speaks to all of, August Wilsons' character Bessie Smith said "we sing the blues not to feel better but to understand life." She is right, music never makes you feel any better about life but it sure can make you see life for all its doom and glory. So my question if I had a chance to ask Bessie is what do you sing when your life is the blues?

I decide that I need to get out, so I change clothes and head up north to do a little dancing. I drive around looking for a parking space and after a while I am ready to give up when someone pulls out and I slide my car right in. I see groups of guys going into a club so I make my way right behind them, yet another club that will have a year on top and be renamed under different owners. I made my way to the bar, placing an order a jack and coke and watch all the sweaty bodies bouncing to the beat. I walk around taking small sips from my glass as a few face intrigues me but none that compel me to speak. A hand grabs my shoulder as I turn to brush them off.

"Remember me?"

Nelson right?

"Yes, how have you been?"

Good and you?

"Fine, you never called."

Sorry about that.

"Wanna dance?"

Sure. I down my drink and I follow Nelson to the dance floor. Nelson reaches back and grabs my hand and only let it go when we reach the dance floor. I look at his thick lips and a smile comes across my face as I imagine his thick red lips gliding across mine. He moves closer to me and I can almost taste the smell of ginger that lingers from his body.

An hour later we walk to the side, as he whispers in my ear how much he wanted to call me. His hand rests on my hand and my body tingles with delight. As I look over his shoulder I spot him, Reggie. He sees me and I realize that I am not ready to move in this direction.

"You want to get out of here?"

I do, but it wouldn't be fair to you.

"Let me be the judge of that."

You are so sexy, damn I want to so bad but it's not going to happen tonight.

"All right but at least have dinner with me."

I can do that.

"Give me your phone." He types his number into my phone and we hug and I walk over to Reggie. My heart is beating so fast, I don't know what to do. He looks at me but doesn't move so I turn and start toward the exit. I can't do this. I can't walk to him; I can't feel what Shaun left me with, not tonight. So I exit the club.

"Gabriel wait. What's wrong?"

Nothing, just tired, heading home.

"Are you sure?"

Yes.

"Stay."

No, I can't but you have a good time.

"Let me go with you."

No! I'm good. Good night Reggie. I turn and walk away sure I had done the right thing.

As I drove up to my place, there he was, sitting on the steps. His eyes lit up as I parked. I tried to control all the emotions that begin to explode inside my body. I still love him and yet I hate him. Life is so damn easy to dig deeper holes for yourself. Love shouldn't be like this all I have asked of love is not dig me any deeper.

"Hey."

What are you doing here?

"I can't come inside?"

There is nothing for us to say that hasn't already been said.

"I never stopped loving you."

That wasn't enough though; your love didn't stop you.

"How many times do I have to apologize, really are we going to do this out here?" We enter and I turn to him.

I need for you to just leave me alone.

"I can never undo what I have done. I love you, I have loved you since the day I looked across that ballroom and saw and I knew that I was meant to spend the rest of my life with you. I fucked up. If you give me a chance I will spend my entire life making this up to you."

I can't. I'm going to take a shower and head to bed, alone. You're rich and famous find a hotel.

I turn on the shower and begin to scrub my body. After a few seconds I feel someone watching me and turn to see Shaun standing in the doorway. He is completely naked. He steps inside the shower with me, placing his arms around me, lifting me into his chest and we begin to kiss. His lips are soothing and his hands ignite parts of my body making me feel awake for the first time in what seemed a long time. He wets my body with his lips below while the water wets my face. He engulfs my manhood and grab on as he lifts me further, in this moment all my anger is gone, all my heartache is gone but the love is gone.

I raise myself off of his arm and reach inside the night stand and grab a pack of cigarettes and stand next to the window and light one.

"You started back?"

Yes.

"You can't forgive me."

No, I don't know.

"It felt different, I never meant…"

…Don't say it; it just makes it hurt more.

"Can I give you some time?"

Don't get me wrong, I still love you, with all my heart but damn this week has been a lot of disappointment for me and I don't know if my heart can survive another one.

"I'll give you some time, some space but I need you to promise me one thing."

What's that?

"That you will at least fight for us."

I can do that. I lay down next to him and he brings me into his body. My heart beat and his melt into each other's and I cry and I feel his tear hits the top of my head. Our love should have lasted forever but it didn't. When is it going to be my turn, two murders and heartbreak maybe I should just give up because life wasn't trying to befriend me, no it was trying to make me its enemy.

Shaun dresses the next morning and I watch from my bed. We both know that this is over, lying together the previous nights, I think our hearts became at peace with this ending. I allow myself to release the anger but I am not able to move forward with him. The room is quiet as he dresses. There is a slight chill in the air as the Lysol sprayer sprays a vanilla scent in the air. What would it say if I allow him to stay in my life? How could I not expect him to do it again, knowing that I allowed it? They say once a cheater, always a cheater. What if it was not true and I was allowing happiness to walk out of my life over a mistake.  Shaun walks to the bed and I rise to meet his embrace. AS we embrace the words of Brownstone plays in my head,

*Now and then I wonder where you are and where you've been. We were friends, but deep inside my heart I always knew, I only needed one not two. I wish I could say the same for you.*

I couldn't say that to Shaun. He squeezes me tighter and I hold on to him, the tears come from both of us. This was hard and part of me wants to tell we can fix this but I can't.

"I will never forgive myself for losing you."

Shaun don't.

"No, I do understand what I am losing. I will always love you." Shaun kisses the top of my head and we move apart and our hands connect and he continues to move farther and farther away from me until we could not touch only look. He exits the room and I lean back and my soul gushes a stream of lost.

I get dress and go pick up my son from my brothers. Brian jumps in my arms and I squeeze him tightly. He is so happy so happy to see me which makes things feel better. Michael asks Kim to take Brian in the back to get his things.

"Dad died yesterday, we tried to call you."

All right.

"Is that all you have to say?" There was anger in his voice and I couldn't quite understand.

What else would you like to hear from me Michael?

"He was your father, whatever else happen between the two of you, your father just died, you can't show any remorse."

He stopped being my father a long time ago. He hated me.

"You have to let that go, for moms' sake."

She made a choice, they both did.

"You don't see how hard it was for him."

You're kidding me right, you know what he said to me, what he did to me.

"So what are you saying?"

He may have died for you yesterday but he died to me before that, I've done my mourning and I'm done.

"I've always been there for you and I need you to do this for this family."

I can't. Brain comes with his bag, I look at Michael and I grab my son by his hand and exit. I am shaking and I can feel Brian grab my hand tighter. I was so angry at Michael for even asking me to come to the man who told me I disgust him. Even on his death bed, he hated me. He couldn't even love at the end.

When I arrive at home a bright smile is there waiting for me. He has some BJ Markets in one hand and RJ in the other. It'll be five years this November that I have returned home and my life has changed in ways then I could have ever imagine. I came home because I had lost a love like no other and it hurt too damn much to live in that city. Since I have been back I had two other loves, maybe neither one of them great but meaningful. Simon could have been great. A part of me always believed it would end where it started. Simon began my soul, Aries grew, Simon revived it and Shaun made it real.

Brian and RJ enter and race up the stairs to his bedroom, Reggie and I enter the kitchen and begin to warm up the food. We don't talk much during this time but it is as natural as possible.
> "So you all right?"
> I'm good.
> "If you need anything."
> I don't. My cell phone begins to ring, I walk over and answer.
> "This is Eric; can you come to the office?"
> In the morning?
> "No, tonight."
> Can it wait, I'm about to have dinner?
> "I wouldn't call if it wasn't priority." I look at Reggie, he tells me to go ahead.
> I'll be there in fifteen minutes. I hang up the phone, grab my jacket and head out the front door.

The drive to the near south side reveals the first signs of winter defrost. It seems even in this evening, all the citizens are trying to take advantage of the warmer night air. The sounds of the city are somehow muted this evening, except for the few car horns and engines from the transits that echo all around. The city was as quiet as the Bears scoring a touchdown on offense. A young couple stood at a bus stop. Her head rested on his chest as she held on to his hand to keep it around, her eyes was close as his were wide open and he stared out into the night. His gray tweed coat covers his long slender body; her blue seemingly thin coat wrapped its way around her. I turn at fourteenth and parked directly off of Wabash and made my way up into the offices of Conurbation.

As enter I see Eric and a man I don't recognize sitting in his office. I enter and take a sit.

What's the emergency? Eric hands me a file and I begin to look through it. Seven bodies all found in Washington Park frozen ponds after the first winter, the last one found this morning, young man twenty two year old William Parker, African American, college student. Missing since January twentieth.

"The truth is we don't know how many boys are connected."

Yes, they are all around the same age, they are all African American males but there is no other connection.

"You grew up around here, you know the area, and everyone talks around what is going on there until some alderman tries to crack down for a minute. If every winter a slew of white boys were murder, all around the same age, in the nearby locations and it occurred every year, there would be no doubt this would be at least a article."

What is it you want from me?

"Let me introduce you to Alan King."

The Alan King?

"No, just Alan. Listen Gabriel, I know your work, the investigative work on corporate corruption Georgia schools; the series you did here on the political corruption and of course the Atlanta murders. I wanted to cover this as a piece in the Tribune but the answer was no from the people on top. Too much time and not enough bang. So I came to Eric."

Where did you get the folder?

"A source inside the CPD."

"Listen Gabe", Eric says, "You are the man for this job, when you came here I gave you a lot of shit stories and you always brought back more than I expected. This is a real story; I need you to take it."

I need to look over the file and talk to your source. I'll also need access to the autopsies.

"Anything you need," Eric says.

Back at home I enter and the house is quiet. I make my way to the kitchen as it is the only light that remains and Reggie stands washing some dishes. I walk over and pick up the dry towel and begin to dry the dishes. I turn to see a weird look over his face.

What's wrong? Reggie turns to me and pulls me into him and he begins to kiss me. My body reacts with such lightening quickness that I cannot do anything but respond as it has already responded in the affirmative.  When he releases me, I look at him.

"It's been damn near five years and we both knew then that there was something there. I've been patient as hell."

You haven't been lonely.

"I said patient, not stupid. Now is our time, I love you dude. I loved you in  some way the first time we shook hands, my soul told me that, but my heart took a little longer to convince and well you know how your ass gets, always got some dude, trying to get at you, I said I would wait my turn, it's our time now. You know it and I know it. You are my best friend and yes it scares me to risk ever losing that but you know what, I am not worried, we, me and you, we are meant to last forever." I said next to him, quiet, not really confused, just waiting. "Say something."

Oh, my turn. I love you Reggie. With that we embraced, our lips touched and the world continued as it did the night before.

Milton Keynes UK
Ingram Content Group UK Ltd.
UKHW030619140324
439439UK00002B/381